THE SQUIRE OF SANDAL-SIDE

A Pastoral Romance

I0667420

AMELIA E. BARR

1st WORLD
LIBRARY
Literary Society

The Squire of Sandal-Side

Amelia E. Barr

© 1st World Library, 2007
PO Box 2211
Fairfield, IA 52556
www.1stworldlibrary.com
First Edition

LCCN: 2007935368

Softcover ISBN: 978-1-4218-9305-1
Hardcover ISBN: 978-1-4218-9405-8
eBook ISBN: 978-1-4218-9205-4

Purchase *"The Squire of Sandal-Side"*
as a traditional bound book at:
www.1stWorldLibrary.com/purchase.asp?ISBN=978-1-4218-9305-1

1st World Library is a literary, educational organization
dedicated to:

- Creating a free internet library of downloadable ebooks

- Hosting writing competitions and offering book publishing
  scholarships.

Interested in more 1st World Library books? contact:
literacy@1stworldlibrary.com
Check us out at: www.1stworldlibrary.com

1ˢᵗ World Library Literary Society

Giving Back to the World

"If you want to work on the core problem, it's early school literacy."

- James Barksdale, former CEO of Netscape

"No skill is more crucial to the future of a child, or to a democratic and prosperous society, than literacy."

- Los Angeles Times

"Literacy... means far more than learning how to read and write... The aim is to transmit... knowledge and promote social participation."

- UNESCO

"Literacy is not a luxury, it is a right and a responsibility. If our world is to meet the challenges of the twenty-first century we must harness the energy and creativity of all our citizens."

- President Bill Clinton

"Parents should be encouraged to read to their children, and teachers should be equipped with all available techniques for teaching literacy, so the varying needs and capacities of individual kids can be taken into account."

- Hugh Mackay

CONTENTS

CHAPTER I

SEAT-SANDAL

"This happy breed of men, this little world."
"To know
That which before us lies in daily life
Is the prime wisdom."
"All that are lovers of virtue ... be quiet, and go a-angling."

There is a mountain called Seat-Sandal, between the Dunmail Raise and Grisedale Pass; and those who have stood upon its summit know that Grasmere vale and lake lie at their feet, and that Windermere, Esthwaite, and Coniston, with many arms of the sea, and a grand brotherhood of mountains, are all around them. There is also an old gray manor-house of the same name. It is some miles distant from the foot of the mountain, snugly sheltered in one of the loveliest valleys between Coniston and Torver. No one knows when the first stones of this house were laid. The Sandals were in Sandal-Side when the white-handed, waxen-faced Edward was building Westminster Abbey, and William the Norman was laying plans for the crown of England. Probably they came with those Norsemen who a century earlier made the Isle of Man their headquarters, and from it, landing on the opposite coast of Cumberland, settled themselves among valleys and lakes and mountains of primeval beauty, which must have strongly reminded them of their native land.

For the prevailing names of this district are all of the Norwegian type, especially such abounding suffixes and prefixes as *seat* from "set," a dwelling; *dale* from "dal," a valley; *fell* from "fjeld," a mountain; *garth* from "gard," an enclosure; and *thwaite*, from "thveit," a clearing. It is certain, also, that, in spite of much Anglo-Saxon admixture, the salt blood of the roving Viking is still in the Cumberland dalesman. Centuries of bucolic isolation have not obliterated it. Every now and then the sea calls some farmer or shepherd, and the restless drop in his veins gives him no peace till he has found his way over the hills and fells to the port of Whitehaven, and gone back to the cradling bosom that rocked his ancestors.

But in the main, this lovely spot was a northern Lotus-land to the Viking. The great hills shut him in from the sight of the sea. He built himself a "seat," and enclosed "thwaites" of greater or less extent; and, forgetting the world in his green paradise, was for centuries almost forgotten by the world. And if long descent and an ancient family have any special claim to be held honorable, it is among the Cumberland "statesmen," or freeholders, it must be looked for in England.

The Sandals have been wise and fortunate owners of the acres which Loegberg Sandal cleared for his descendants. They have a family tradition that he came from Iceland in his own galley; and a late generation has written out portions of a saga,—long orally transmitted,—which relates the incidents of his voyage. All the Sandals believe implicitly in its authenticity; and, indeed, though it is full of fighting, of the plunder of gold and rich raiment, and the carrying off of fair women, there is nothing improbable in its relations, considering the people and the time whose story it professes to tell.

Doubtless this very Loegberg Sandal built the central hall of Seat-Sandal. There were giants in those days; and it must have been the hands of giants that piled the massive blocks, and eyes accustomed to great expanses that measured off the large and lofty space. Smaller rooms have been built above it and around it, and every generation has added something to its beauty and comfort; but Loegberg's great hall, with its enormous fireplace, is still the heart of the home.

For nowhere better than among these "dalesmen" can the English elemental resistance to fusion be seen. Only at the extreme point of necessity have they exchanged ideas with any other section, yet they have left their mark all over English history. In Cumberland and Westmoreland, the most pathetic romances of the Red Rose were enacted. In the strength of these hills, the very spirit of the Reformation was cradled. From among them came the Wyckliffite queen of Henry the Eighth, and the noble confessor and apostle Bernard Gilpin. No lover of Protestantism can afford to forget the man who refused the bishopric of Carlisle, and a provostship at Oxford, that he might traverse the hills and dales, and read to the simple "statesmen" and shepherds the unknown Gospels in the vernacular. They gathered round him in joyful wonder, and listened kneeling to the Scriptures. Only the death of Mary prevented his martyrdom; and to-day his memory is as green as are the ivies and sycamores around his old home.

The Protestant spirit which Gilpin raised among these English Northmen was exceptionally intense; and here George Fox found ready the strong mystical element neces- sary for his doctrines. For these men had long worshipped "in temples not made with hands." In the solemn "high places" they had learned to interpret the voices of winds and waters; and among the stupendous crags, more like clouds at sunset than fragments of solid land, they had seen and heard wonderful things. All over this country, from Kendal to old Ulverston, Fox was known and loved; and from Swarthmoor Hall, a manor-house not very far from Seat-Sandal, he took his wife.

After this the Stuarts came marching through the dales, but the followers of Wyckliffe and Fox had little sympathy with the Stuarts. In the rebellion of 1715, their own lord, the Earl of Derwentwater, was beheaded for aiding the unfortunate family; and the hills and waters around are sad with the memories of his lady's heroic efforts and sufferings. So, when Prince Charles came again, in 1745, they were moved neither by his beauty nor his romantic daring: they would take no part at all in his brilliant blunder.

It was for his stanch loyalty on this occasion, that the Christopher Sandal of that day was put among the men whom King George determined to honor. A baronetcy was offered him, which he declined; for he had a feeling that he would deeply offend old Loegberg Sandal, and perhaps all the rest of his ancestral wraiths, if he merged their ancient name in that of Baron of Torver. The sentiment was one the German King of England could understand and respect; and Sandal received, in place of a costly title, the lucrative office of High Sheriff of Cumberland, and a good share besides of the forfeited lands of the rebel houses of Huddleston and Millom.

Then he took his place among the great county families of England. He passed over his own hills, and went up to London, and did homage for the king's grace to him. And that strange journey awakened in the mountain lord some old spirit of adventure and curiosity. He came home by the

Amelia E. Barr

ocean, and perceived that he had only half lived before. He sent his sons to Oxford; he made them travel; he was delighted when the youngest two took to the sea as naturally as the eider-ducks fledged in a sea-sand nest.

Good fortune did not spoil the old, cautious family. It went "cannily" forward, and knew how "to take occasion by the hand," and how to choose its friends. Towards the close of the eighteenth century, an opportune loan again set the doors of the House of Lords open to the Sandals; but the head of the family was even less inclined to enter it than his grandfather had been.

"Nay, then," was his answer, "t' Sandals are too old a family to hide their heads in a coronet. Happen, I am a bit opinion-tied, but it's over late to loosen knots made centuries ago; and I don't want to loosen them, neither."

So it will be perceived, that, though the Sandals moved, they moved slowly. A little change went a great way with them. The men were all conservative in politics, the women intensely so in all domestic traditions. They made their own sweet waters and unguents and pomades, long after the nearest chemist supplied a far better and cheaper article. Their spinning-wheels hummed by the kitchen-fire, and their shuttles glided deftly in the weaving-room, many a year after Manchester cottons were cheap and plentiful. But they were pleasant, kindly women, who did wonderful needlework, and made all kinds of dainty dishes and cordials and sirups. They were famous florists and gardeners, and the very neatest of housewives. They visited the poor and sick, and never went empty-handed. They were hearty Churchwomen. They loved God, and were truly pious, and were hardly aware of it; for those were not days of much inquiry. People did their duty and were happy, and did not reason as to "why" they did it, nor try to ascertain if there were a legitimate cause for the effect.

But about the beginning of this century, a different day began to dawn over Sandal-Side. The young heir came to his own, and signalized the event by marrying the rich Miss Lowther of Whitehaven. She had been finely educated. She had lived in large cities, and been to court. She dressed elegantly; she had a piano and much grand furniture brought over the hills to Sandal; and she filled the old house during the summer with lords and ladies, and poets and artists, who flitted about the idyllic little village, like gay butterflies in a lovely garden.

The husband and children of such a woman were not likely to stand still. Sandal, encouraged by her political influence, went into Parliament. Her children did fairly well; for though one boy was wild, and cost them a deal of money, and another went away in a passion one morning, and never came back, the heir was a good son, and the two girls made splendid marriages. On the whole, she could feel that she had done well to her generation. Even after she had been long dead, the old women in the village talked of her beauty and spirit, of the tight hand she kept over every one and every thing pertaining to Sandal. Of all the mistresses of the old "seat," this Mistress Charlotte was the most prominent and the best remembered.

Every one who steps within the wide, cool hall of Seat-Sandal faces first of all things her picture. It is a life-size painting of a beautiful woman, in the queer, scant costume of the regency. She wears a white satin frock and white satin slippers, and carries in her hand a bunch of white roses. She appears to be coming down a flight of wide stairs; one foot is lifted for the descent, and the dark background, and the dim light in which it hangs, give to the illusion an almost startling reality. It was her fancy to have the painting hung there to welcome all who entered her doors; and though it is now old-fashioned, and rather shabby and faded, no one of the present generation cares to order its removal. All hold quietly to the opinion that "grandmother would not like it."

In that quiet acre on the hillside, which holds the generations of the Sandals, she had been at rest for ten years. But her son still bared his gray head whenever he passed her picture; still, at times, stood a minute before it, and said with tender respect, "I salute thee, mother." And in her granddaughter's lives still she interfered; for she had left in their father's charge a sum of money, which was to be used solely to give them some pleasure which they could not have without it. In this way, though dead, she kept herself a part of their young lives; became a kind of fairy grandmother, who gave them only delightful things, and her name continued a household word.

Only the mother seemed averse to speak it; and Charlotte, who was most observant, noticed that she never lifted her eyes to the picture as she passed it. There were reasons for these things which the children did not understand. They had been too young at her death to estimate the bondage in which she had kept her daughter-in-law, who, for her husband's sake, had been ever patient and reticent. Nothing is, indeed, more remarkable than the patience of wives under this particular trial. They may be restive under many far less wrongs, but they bear the mother-in-law grievance with a dignity which shames the grim joking and the petulant abuse of men towards the same relationship. And for many years the young wife had borne nobly a domestic tyranny which pressed her on every hand. If then, she was glad to be set free from it, the feeling was too natural to be severely blamed; for she never said so,—no, not even by a look. Her children had the benefit of their grandmother's kindness, and she was too honorable to deprive the dead of their meed of gratitude.

The present holder of Sandal had none of his mother's

ambitious will. He cared for neither political nor fashionable life; and as soon as he came to his inheritance, married a handsome, sensible daleswoman with whom he had long been in love. Then he retired from a world which had nothing to give him comparable, in his eyes, with the simple, dignified pleasures incident to his position as Squire of Sandal-Side. For dearly he loved the old hall, with its sheltering sycamores and oaks,—oaks which had been young trees when the knights lying in Furness Abbey led the Grasmere bowmen at Crecy and Agincourt. Dearly he loved the large, low rooms, full of comfortable elegance; and the sweet, old-fashioned, Dutch garden, so green through all the snows of winter, so cheerfully grave and fragrant in the summer twilights, so shady and cool even in the hottest noons.

Thirty years ago he was coming through it one July evening. It had been a very hot day; and the flowers were drooping, and the birds weary and silent. But Squire Sandal, though flushed and rumpled looking, had still the air of drippy mornings and hazy afternoons about him. There was a creel at his back, and a fishing-rod in his hand, and he had just come from the high, unplanted places, and the broomy, breezy moorlands; and his broad, rosy face expressed nothing but happiness.

At his side walked his favorite daughter Charlotte,—his dear companion, the confidant and sharer of all his sylvan pleasures. She was tired and dusty; and her short printed gown showed traces of green, spongy grass, and lichen-covered rocks. But her face was a joy to see: she had such bright eyes, such a kind, handsome mouth, such a cheerful voice, such a merry laugh. As they came in sight of the wide-open front-doors, she looked ruefully down at her feet and her grass-and-water-stained skirt, and then into her father's face.

Amelia E. Barr

"I don't know what Sophia will say if she sees me, father; I don't, indeed."

"Never you mind her, dear. Sophia's rather high, you know. And we've had a rare good time. Eh? What?"

"I should think we have! There are not many pleasures in life better than persuading a fine trout to go a little way down stream with you. Are there, father?"

"You are right, Charlotte. Trout are the kind of company you want on an outing. And then, you know, if you can only persuade one to go down stream a bit with you, there's not much difficulty in persuading him to let you have the pleasure of seeing him to dinner. Eh? What?"

"I think I will go round by the side-door, father. I might meet some one in the hall."

"Nay, don't do that. There isn't any need to shab off. You've done nothing wrong, and I'm ready to stand by you, my dear; and you know what a good time we've been having all day. Eh? What?"

"Of course I know, father,—

"Showers and clouds and winds,
All things well and proper;
Trailer, red and white,
Dark and wily dropper.
Midges true to fling
Made of plover hackle,
With a gaudy wing,
And a cobweb tackle."

"Cobweb tackle, eh, Charlotte? Yes, certainly; for a hand

that can manage it. Lancie Crossthwaite will land you a trout, three pounds weight, with a line that wouldn't lift a dead weight of one pound from the floor to the table. I'll uphold he will. Eh? What?"

"I'll do it myself, some day; see if I don't, father."

"I've no doubt of it, Charlotte; not a bit." Then being in the entrance-hall, they parted with a smile of confidence, and Charlotte hastened up-stairs to prepare herself for the evening meal. She gave one quick glance at her grand-mother's picture as she passed it, a glance of mingled deprecation and annoyance; for there were times when the complacent serenity of the perfect face, and the perfect propriety of the white satin gown, gave her a little spasm of indignation.

She dressed rapidly, with a certain deft grace that was part of her character. And it was a delightful surprise to watch the metamorphosis; the more so, as it went on with a perfect unconsciousness of its wonderful beauty. Here a change, and there a change, until the bright brown hair was loosened from its net of knotted silk, to fall in wavy, curly masses; and the printed gown was exchanged for one of the finest muslin, pink and flowing, and pinned together with bows of pale blue satin. A daring combination, which precisely suited her blonde, brilliant beauty. Her eyes were shining; her cheeks touched by the sun till they had the charming tints of a peach on a southern wall. She looked at herself with a little nod of satisfaction, and then tapped at the door of the room adjoining her own. It was Miss Sandal's room; and Miss Sandal, though only sixteen months older than Charlotte, exacted all the deference due to her by the right of primogeniture.

"Come in, Charlotte."

"How did you know it was I?"

"I know your knock, however you vary it. Nobody knocks like you. I suppose no two people would make three taps just the same." She was far too polite to yawn; but she made as much of the movement as she could not control, and then put a mark in her book, and laid it down. A very different girl, indeed, was she from her younger sister; a stranger would never have suspected her of the same parentage.

She had dark, fine eyes, which, however, did not express what she felt: they rather gave the idea of storing up impressions to be re-acted upon by some interior power. She had a delicate complexion, a great deal of soft, black hair compactly dressed, and a neat figure. Her disposition was dreamy and self-willed; occult studies fascinated her, and she was passionately fond of moonlight. She was simply dressed in a white muslin frock, with a black ribbon around her slim waist; but the ribbon was clasped by a buckle of heavily chased gold, and her fingers had many rings on them, and looked—a very rare circumstance—the better for them. Having put down her book, she rose from her chair; and as she dipped the tips of her hands in water, and wiped them with elaborate nicety, she talked to Charlotte in a soft, deliberate way.

"Where have you been, you and father, ever since daybreak?"

"Up to Blaeberry Tarn, and then home by Holler Beck. We caught a creel full of trout, and had a very happy day."

"Really, you know?"

"Yes, really; why not?"

"I cannot understand it, Charlotte. I suppose we never were sisters before." She said the words with the air of one who rather states a fact than asks a question; and Charlotte, not at all comprehending, looked at her curiously and interrogatively.

"I mean that our relationship in this life does not touch our anterior lives."

"Oh, you know you are talking nonsense, Sophia! It gives me such a feel, you can't tell, to think of having lived before; and I don't believe it. There, now! Come, dear, let us go to dinner; I'm that hungry I'm fit to drop." For Charlotte was watching, with a feeling of injury, Sophia's leisurely method of putting every book and chair and hairpin in its place.

The sisters' rooms were precisely alike in their general features, and yet there was as great a relative difference in their apartments as in their natures. Both were large, low rooms, facing the sunrise. The walls of both were of dark oak; the roofs of both were of the same sombre wood; so also were the floors. They were literally oak chambers. And in both rooms the draperies of the beds, chairs, and windows were of white dimity. But in Sophia's, there were many pictures, souvenirs of girlhood's friendships, needlework, finished and unfinished drawings, and a great number of books mostly on subjects not usually attractive to young women. Charlotte's room had no pictures on its walls, and no odds and ends of memorials; and as sewing was to her a duty and not a pleasure, there was no crotcheting or Berlin-wool work in hand; and with the exception of a handsome copy of "Izaak Walton," there were no books on her table but a Bible, Book of Common Prayer, and a very shabby Thomas a Kempis.

So dissimilar were the girls in their appearance and their

tastes; and yet they loved each other with that calm, habitual, family affection, which, undemonstrative as it is, stands the wear and tug of life with a wonderful tenacity. Down the broad, oak stairway they sauntered together; Charlotte's tall, erect figure, bright, loose hair, pink dress, and flowing ribbons, throwing into effective contrast the dark hair, dark eyes, white drapery, and gleaming ornaments of her elder sister.

In the hall they met the squire. He was very fond and very proud of his daughters; and he gave his right arm to Sophia, and slipped his left hand into Charlotte's hand with an affectionate pride and confidence that was charming.

"Any news, mother?" he asked, as he lifted one of the crisp brown trout from its bed of white damask and curly green parsley.

"None, squire; only the sheep-shearing at the Up-Hill Farm to-morrow. John of Middle Barra called with the statesman's respects. Will you go, squire?"

"Certainly. My men are all to lend a hand. Barf Latrigg is ageing fast now; he was my father's crony; if I slighted him, I should feel as if father knew about it. Which of you will go with me? Thou, mother?"

"That, I cannot, squire. The servant lasses are all promised for the fleece-folding; and it's a poor house that won't keep one woman busy in it."

"Sophia and Charlotte will go then?"

"Excuse me, father," answered Sophia languidly. "I shall have a headache to-morrow, I fear; I have been nervous and poorly all the afternoon."

"Why, Sophia, I didn't think I had such a foolish lass! Taking fancies for she doesn't know what. If you plan for to-morrow, plan a bit of pleasure with it; that's a long way better than expecting a headache. Charlotte will go then. Eh? What?"

"Yes, father; I will go. Sophia never could bear walking in the heat. I like it; and I think there are few things merrier than a sheep-shearing."

"So poetic! So idyllic!" murmured Sophia, with mild sarcasm.

"Many people think so, Sophia. Mr. Wordsworth would remember Pan and Arcadian shepherds playing on reedy pipes, and Chaldaean shepherds studying the stars, and those on Judaea's hills who heard the angels singing. He would think of wild Tartar shepherds, and handsome Spanish and Italian."

"And still handsomer Cumberland ones." And Sophia, having given this little sisterly reminder, added calmly, "I met Mr. Wordsworth to-day, father. He had come over the fells with a party, and he looked very much bored with his company."

"I shouldn't wonder if he were. He likes his own company best. He is a great man now, but I remember well when people thought he was just a little off-at-side. You knew Nancy Butterworth, mother?"

"Certainly I did, squire. She lived near Rydal."

"Yes. Nancy wasn't very bright herself. A stranger once asked her what Mr. Wordsworth was like; and she said, 'He's canny enough at times. Mostly he's wandering up and down t' hills, talking his po-et-ry; but now and then he'll say, "How do ye do, Nancy?" as sensible as you or me.'"

"Mr. Wordsworth speaks foolishness to a great many people besides Nancy Butterworth," said Sophia warmly; "but he is a great poet and a great seer to those who can understand him."

"Well, well, Mr. Wordsworth is neither here nor there in our affairs. We'll go up to Latriggs in the afternoon, Charlotte. I'll be ready at two o'clock."

"And I, also, father." Her face was flushed and thoughtful, and she had become suddenly quiet. The squire glanced at her, but without curiosity; he only thought, "What a pity she is a lass! I wish Harry had her good sense and her good heart; I do that."

CHAPTER II

THE SHEEP-SHEARING

"Plain living and high thinking ...
The homely beauty of the good old cause,
...our peace, our fearful innocence,
And pure religion breathing household laws."

"A happy youth, and their old age
Is beautiful and free."

The sheep-shearings at Up-Hill Farm were a kind of rural Olympics. Shepherds came there from far and near to try their skill against each other,—young men in their prime mostly, with brown, ruddy faces, and eyes of that bright blue lustre which is only gained by a free, open-air life. The hillside was just turning purple with heather bloom, and along the winding, stony road the yellow asphodels were dancing in the wind. Everywhere there was the scent of bog-myrtle and wild-rose and sweetbrier, and the tinkling sound of becks babbling over glossy rocks; and in the glorious sunshine and luminous air, the mountains appeared to expand and elevate, and to throw out glowing peaks and summits into infinite space.

Hand in hand the squire and his daughter climbed the fellside. They had left home in high spirits, merrily flinging back the mother's and Sophia's last advices; but gradually they became silent, and then a little mournful. "I wonder why it is, father?" asked Charlotte; "I'm not at all tired, and how can fresh air and sunshine make one melancholy?"

"Maybe, now, sad thoughts are catching. I was having a few. Eh? What?"

"I don't know. Why were you having sad thoughts?"

"Well, then, I really can't understand why. There's no need to fret over changes. At the long end the great change puts all right. Charlotte, I have been coming to Barf Latrigg's shearings for about half a century. I remember the first. I held my nurse's hand, and wore such a funny little coat, and such a big lace collar. And, dear me! it was just such a day as this, thirty-two years ago, that your mother walked up to the shearing with me, Charlotte; and I asked her if she would be my wife, and she said she would. Thou takes after her a good deal; she had the very same bright eyes and bonny face, and straight, tall shape thou has to-day. Barf Latrigg was sixty then, turning a bit gray, but able to shear with any man they could put against him. He'll be ninety now; but his father lived till he was more than a hundred, and most of his fore-elders touched the century. He's had his troubles too."

"I never heard of them."

"No. They are dead and buried. A dead trouble may be forgot: it is the living troubles that make the eyes dim, and the heart fail. Yes, yes; Barf is as happy as a boy now, but I remember when he was back-set and fore-set with trouble. In life every thing goes round like a cart-wheel. Eh? What?"

In a short time they reached the outer wall of the farm. They were eight hundred feet above the valley; and looking backwards upon the woods from their airy shelf, the tops of the trees appeared like a solid green road, on which they might drop down and walk. Stone steps in the stone wall admitted them into the enclosure, and then they saw the low gray house spreading itself in the shadow of the noble sycamores—

... "musical with bees;
Such tents the patriarchs loved."

As they approached, the old statesman strode to the open door to meet them. He was a very tall man, with a bright, florid face, and a great deal of fine, white hair. Two large sheep-dogs, which only wanted a hint to be uncivil, walked beside him. He had that independent manner which honorable descent and absolute ownership of house and land give; and he looked every inch a gentleman, though he wore only the old dalesman's costume,—breeches of buckskin fastened at the knees with five silver buttons, home-knit stockings and low shoes, and a red waistcoat, open that day, in order to show the fine ruffles on his shirt. He was precisely what Squire Sandal would have been, if the Sandals had not been forced by circumstances into contact with a more cultivated and a more ambitious life.

"Welcome, Sandal! I have been watching for thee. There would be little prosperation in a shearing if thou wert absent. And a good day to thee, Charlotte. My Ducie was speaking of thee a minute ago. Here she comes to help thee off with thy things."

Charlotte was untying her bonnet as she entered the deep, cool porch, and a moment afterward Ducie was at her side. It was easy to see the women loved each other, though Ducie only smiled, and said, "Come in; I'm right glad to see you, Charlotte. Come into t' best room, and cool your face a bit. And how is Mrs. Sandal and Sophia? Be things at their usual, dear?"

"Thank you, Ducie; all and every thing is well,—I hope. We have not heard from Harry lately. I think it worrits father a little, but he is never the one to show it. Oh, how sweet this room is!"

She was standing before the old-fashioned swivel mirror, that had reflected three generations,—a fair, bright girl, with the light and hope of youth in her face. The old room, with its oak walls, immense bed, carved awmries, drawers, and cupboards, made a fine environment for so much life and color. And yet there were touches in it that resembled her, and seemed to be the protest of the present with the past,— vivid green and scarlet masses of geranium and fuchsia in the latticed window, and a great pot of odorous flowers upon the hearthstone. But the peculiar sweetness which Charlotte noticed came from the polished oak floor, which was strewed with bits of rosemary and lavender, to prevent the slipping of the feet upon it.

Charlotte looked down at them as she ejaculated, "How sweet this room is!" and the shadow of a frown crossed her face. "I would not do it, Ducie, for any one," she said. "Poor herbs of grace! What sin have they committed to be trodden under foot? I would not do it, Ducie: I feel as if it hurt them."

"Nay, now; flowers grow to be pulled dear, just as lasses grow to be loved and married."

"Is that what you think, Ducie? Some cherished in the jar; some thrown under the feet, and bruised to death,—the feet of wrong and sorrow,"—

"Don't you talk that way, Charlotte. It isn't lucky for girls to talk of wrong and sorrow. Talking of things bespeaks them. There's always *them* that hear; *them* that we don't see. And everybody pulls flowers, dearie."

"I don't. If I pull a rose, I always believe every other rose on that tree is sad about it. They may be in families, Ducie, who can tell? And the little roses may be like the little children, and very dear to the grown roses."

"Why, what fancies! Let us go into the yard, and see the shearing. You've made me feel as if I'd never like to pull a posy again. You shouldn't say such things, indeed you shouldn't: you've given me quite a turn, I'm sure."

As Ducie talked, they went through the back-door into a large yard walled in from the hillside, and having in it three grand old sycamores. One of these was at the top of the enclosure, and a circle of green shadow like a tent was around it. In this shadow the squire and the statesman were sitting. Their heads were uncovered, their long clay pipes in their hands; and, with a placid complacency, they were watching the score of busy men before them. Many had come long distances to try their skill against each other; for the shearings at Latrigg's were a pastoral game, at which it was a local honor to be the winner. There the young statesman who could shear his six score a day found others of a like capacity, and it was Greek against Greek at Up-Hill shearing that afternoon.

"I had two thousand sheep to get over," said Latrigg, "but they'll be bare by sunset, squire. That isn't bad for these days. When I was young we wouldn't have thought so much of two thousand, but every dalesman then knew what good shearing was. *Now*," and the old man shook his head slowly, "good shearers are few and far between. Why, there's some here from beyond Kirkstone Pass and Nab Scar!"

It was customary for young people of all conditions to give men as aged as Barf Latrigg the honorable name of "grandfather;" and Charlotte said, as she sat down in the breezy shadow beside him, "Who is first, grandfather?"

"Why, our Stephen, to be sure! They'll have to be up before day-dawn to keep sidey with our Steve.—Steve, how many is thou ahead now?" The voice that asked the question, though full of triumph, was thin and weak; but the answer came back in full, mellow tones,—

"Fifteen ahead, grandfather."

"Oh, I'm so glad!"

"Charlotte Sandal says 'she's so glad.' Now then, if thou loses ground, I wouldn't give a ha'penny for thee."

Then the women who were folding the fleeces on tables under the other two sycamores lifted their eyes, and glanced at Steve; and some of the elder ones sent him a merry jibe, and some of the younger ones, smiles, that made his brown handsome face deepen in color; but he was far too earnest in his work to spare a moment for a reply. By and by, the squire put down his pipe, and sat watching with his hands upon his knees. And a stray child crept up to Charlotte, and climbed upon her lap, and went to sleep there, and the wind flecked these four representatives of four generations all over with wavering shadows; and Ducie came backwards and forwards, and finally carried the sleeping child into the house; and Stephen, busy as he was, saw every thing that went on in the group under the top sycamore.

Even before sundown, the last batch of sheep were fleeced

and *smitten*,[Smitten. Marked with the cipher of the owner in a mixture mostly of tar.] and turned on to the hillside; and Charlotte, leaning over the wall, watched them wander contentedly up the fell, with their lambs trotting beside them. Grandfather and the squire had gone into the house; Ducie was calling her from the open door; she knew it was tea-time, and she was young and healthy and hungry enough to be glad of it.

At the table she met Stephen. The strong, bare-armed Hercules, whom she had watched tossing the sheep around for his shears as easily as if they had been kittens under his hands, was now dressed in a handsome tweed suit, and looking quite as much of a gentleman as the most fastidious maiden could desire. He came in after the meal had begun, flushed somewhat with his hard labor, and perhaps, also, with the hurry of his toilet; but there was no embarrassment in his manner. It had never yet entered Stephen's mind that there was any occasion for embarrassment, for the friendship between the squire's family and his own had been devoid of all sense of inequality. The squire was "the squire," and was perhaps richer than Latrigg, but even that fact was uncertain; and the Sandals had been to court, and married into county families; but then the Latriggs had been for exactly seven hundred years the neighbors of Sandal,—good neighbors, shoulder to shoulder with them in every trial or emergency.

The long friendship had never known but one temporary shadow, and this had been during the time that the present squire's mother ruled in Sandal; the Mistress Charlotte whose influence was still felt in the old seat. She had entirely disapproved the familiar affection with which Latrigg met her husband, and it was said the disputes which drove one of her sons from his home were caused by her determination to break up the companionship existing between the young people of the two houses at that time.

The squire remembered it. He had also, in some degree, regarded his mother's prejudices while she lived; but, after her death, Sophia and Charlotte, as well as their brother, began to go very often to Up-Hill Farm. Naturally Stephen, who was Ducie's son, became the companion of Harry Sandal; and the girls grew up in his sight like two beautiful sisters. It was only within the past year that he had begun to understand that one was dearer to him than the other; but though none of the three was now ignorant of the fact, it was as yet tacitly ignored. The knowledge had not been pleasant to Sophia; and to Charlotte and Stephen it was such a delicious uncertainty, that they hardly desired to make it sure; and they imagined their secret was all their own, and were so happy in it, that they feared to look too curiously into their happiness.

There was to be a great feast and dance that night: and, as they sat at the tea-table, they heard the mirth and stir of its preparation; but it came into the room only like a pleasant echo, mingling with the barking of the sheep-dogs, and the bleating of the shorn sheep upon the fells, and the murmur of their quiet conversation about "the walks" Latrigg owned, and the scrambling, black-faced breed whose endurance made them so profitable. Something was also said of other shearings to which Stephen must go, if he would assure his claim to be "top-shearer," and of the wool-factories which the most astute statesmen were beginning to build.

"If I were a younger man, I'd be in with them," said Latrigg. "I'd spin and weave my own fleeces, and send them to Leeds market, with no go-between to share my profits." And Steve put in a sensible word now and then, and passed the berry-cake and honey and cream; and withal met Charlotte's eyes, and caught her smiles, and was as happy as love and hope could make him.

After tea the squire wished to go; but Latrigg said, "Smoke one pipe with me Sandal," and they went into the porch together. Then Steve and Charlotte sauntered about the garden, or, leaning on the stone wall, looked down into the valley, or away off to the hills. Many things they said to each other which seemed to mean so little, but which meant so much when love was the interpreter. For Charlotte was eighteen and Stephen twenty-two; and when mortals still so young are in love, they are quite able to create worlds out of nothing.

After a while the squire lifted his eyes, and took in the bit of landscape which included them. The droop of the young heads towards each other, and their air of happy confidence, awakened a vague suspicion in his heart. Perhaps Latrigg was conscious of it; for he said, as if in answer to the squire's thought, "Steve will have all that is mine. It's a deal easier to die, Sandal, when you have a fine lad like Steve to leave the old place to."

"Steve is in the female line. That's a deal different to having sons. Lasses are cold comfort for sons. Eh? What?"

"To be sure; but I've given Steve my name. Any one not called Latrigg at Up-Hill would seem like a stranger."

"I know how you feel about that. A squire in Seat-Sandal out of the old name would have a very middling kind of time, I think. He'd have a sight of ill-will at his back."

"Thou means with *them*!"

The squire nodded gravely; and after a minute's silence said, "It stands to reason *they* take an interest. I do in them. When I think of this or that Sandal, or when I look up at their faces as I sit smoking beside them, I'm sure I feel like their son;

and I wouldn't grieve them any more than if they were to be seen and talked to. It's none likely, then, that *they* forget. I know they don't."

"I'm quite of thy way of thinking, Sandal; but Steve will be called Latrigg. He has never known any other name, thou sees."

"To be sure. Is Ducie willing?"

"Poor lass! She never names Steve's father. He'd no business in her life, and he very soon went out of it. Stray souls will get into families they have no business in, sometimes. They make a deal of unhappiness when they do."

Sandal sat listening with a sympathetic face. He hoped Latrigg was going to tell him something definite about his daughter's trouble; but the old man puffed, puffed, in silence a few minutes, and then turned the conversation. However, Sandal had been touched on a point where he was exceedingly sensitive; and he rose with a sigh, and said, "Well, well, Latrigg, good-by. I'll go down the fell now. Come, Charlotte."

Unconsciously he spoke with an authority not usual to him, and the parting was a little silent and hurried; for Ducie was in the throng of her festival, and rather impatient for Stephen's help. Only Latrigg walked to the gate with them. He looked after Sandal and his daughter with a grave, but not unhappy wistfulness; and when a belt of larches hid them from his view, he turned towards the house, saying softly,—

"It is like to be my last shearing. Very soon this life will *have been*, but through Christ's mercy I have the over-hand of the future."

It was almost as hard to go down the fell as to come up it, for the road was very steep and stony. The squire took it leisurely, carrying his straw hat in his hand, and often standing still to look around him. The day had been very warm; and limpid vapors hung over the mountains, like something far finer than mist,—like air made visible,— giving them an appearance of inconceivable remoteness, full of grandeur; for there is a sublimity of distance, as well as a sublimity of height. He made Charlotte notice them. "Maybe, many a year after this, you'll see the hills look just that way, dearie; then think on this evening and on me."

She did not speak, but she looked into his face, and clasped his hand tightly. She was troubled with her own mood. Try as she would, it was impossible to prevent herself drifting into most unusual silences. Stephen's words and looks filled her heart; she had only half heard the things her father had been saying. Never before had she found an hour in her life when she wished for solitude in preference to his society,— her good, tender father. She put Stephen out of her mind, and tried again to feel all her old interest in his plans for their amusement. Alas, alas! The first secret, especially if it be a love-secret, makes a break in that sweet, confidential intercourse between a parent and child which nothing restores. The squire hardly comprehended that there might be a secret. Charlotte was unthoughtful of wrong; but still there was a repression, a something undefinable between them, impalpable, but positive as a breath of polar air. She noticed the mountains, for he made her do so; but the birds sang sleepy songs to her unheeded, and the yellow asphodels made a kind of sunshine at her feet that she never saw; and even her father's voice disturbed the dreamy charm of thoughts that touched a deeper, sweeter joy than moor or mountain, bird or flower, had ever given her.

Before they reached home, the squire had also become silent.

Amelia E. Barr

He came into the hall with the face of one dissatisfied and unhappy. The feeling spread through the house, as a drop of ink spreads itself through a glass of water. It almost suited Sophia's mood, and Mrs. Sandal was not inclined to discuss it until the squire was alone with her. Then she asked the question of all questions the most irritating, "What is the matter with you, squire?"

"What is the matter, indeed? Love-making. That is the matter, Alice."

"Charlotte?"

"Yes."

"And Stephen Latrigg?"

"Yes."

"I thought as much. Opportunity is a dangerous thing."

"My word! To hear you talk, one would think it was matterless how our girls married."

"It is never matterless how any girl marries, squire; and our Charlotte"—

"Oh, I thought Charlotte was a child yet! How could I tell there was danger at Up-Hill? You ought to have looked better after your daughters. See that she doesn't go near-hand Latrigg's again."

"I wouldn't be so foolish, William. It's a deal better not to notice. Make no words about it; and, if you don't like Stephen, send Charlotte away a bit. Half of young people's love-affairs is just because they are handy to each other."

"'Like Stephen!' It is more than a matter of liking, as you know very well. If Harry Sandal goes on as he has been going, there will be little enough left for the girls; and they must marry where money will not be wanted. More than that, I've been thinking of brother Tom's boy for one of them. Eh? What?"

"You mean, you have been writing to Tom about a marriage? I would have been above a thing like that, William. I suppose you did it to please your mother. She always did hanker after Tom, and she always did dislike the Latriggs. I have heard that when people were in the grave they 'ceased from troubling,' but"—

"Alice!"

"I meant no harm, squire, I'm sure; and I would not say wrong of the dead for any thing, specially of your mother; but I think about my own girls."

"There, now, Alice, don't whimper and cry. I am not going to harm your girls, not I. Only mother was promised that Tom's son should have the first chance for their favor. I'm sure there's nothing amiss in that. Eh?"

"A young man born in a foreign country among blacks, or very near blacks. And nobody knows who his mother was."

"Oh, yes! his mother was a judge's daughter, and she had a deal of money. Her son has been well done to; sent to the very best German and French schools, and now he is at Oxford. I dare say he is a very good young man, and at any rate he is the only Sandal of this generation except our own boy."

"Your sisters have sons."

"Yes, Mary has three: they are *Lockerbys*. Elizabeth has two: they are *Piersons*. My poor brother Launcie was drowned, and never had son or daughter; so that Tom's Julius is the nearest blood we have."

"Julius! I never heard tell of such a name."

"Yes, it is a silly kind of a foreign name. His mother is called Julia: I suppose that is how it comes. No Sandal was ever called such a name before, but the young man mustn't be blamed for his godfather's foolishness, Alice. Eh?"

"I'm not so unjust. Poor Launcie! I saw him once at a ball in Kendal. Are you sure he was drowned?"

"I followed him to Whitehaven, and found out that he had gone away in a ship that never came home. Mother and Launcie were in bad bread when he left, and she never fretted for him as she did for Tom."

"Why did you not tell me all this before?"

"I said to myself, there's time enough yet to be planning husbands for girls that haven't a thought of the kind. We were very happy with them; I couldn't bear to break things up; and I never once feared about Steve Latrigg, not I."

"What does your brother and his wife say?"

"Tom is with me. As for his wife, I know nothing of her, and she knows nothing of us. She has been in England a good many times, but she never said she would like to come and see us, and my mother never wanted to see her; so there wasn't a compliment wasted, you see. Eh? What?"

"No, I don't see, William. All about it is in a muddle, and I must say I never heard tell of such ways. It is like offering your own flesh and blood for sale. And to people who want nothing to do with us. I'm astonished at you, squire."

"Don't go on so, Alice. Tom and I never had any falling out. He just got out of the way of writing. He likes India, and he had his own reasons for not liking England in any shape you could offer England to him. There's no back reckonings between Tom and me, and he'll be glad for Julius to come to his own people. We will ask Julius to Sandal; and you say, yourself, that the half of young folks' loving is in being handy to each other. Eh? What?"

"I never thought you would bring my words up that way. But I'll tell you one thing, my girls are not made of melted wax, William. You'll be a wise man, and a strong man, if you get a ring on their fingers, if they don't want it there. Sophia will say very soft and sweet, 'No, thank you, father;' and you'll move Scawfell and Langdale Pikes before you get her beyond it. As for Charlotte, you yourself will stand 'making' better than she will. And you know that nothing short of an earthquake can lift you an inch outside your own way."

And perhaps Sandal thought the hyperbole a compliment; for he smiled a little, and walked away, with what his wife privately called "a peacocky air," saying something about "Greek meeting Greek" as he did so. Mrs. Sandal did not in the least understand him: she wondered a little over the remark, and then dismissed it as "some of the squire's foolishness."

CHAPTER III

JULIUS SANDAL

"Variety's the very spice of life
That gives it all its flavor."

"Domestic happiness, thou only bliss
Of Paradise that has survived the fall."

Life has a chronology quite independent of the almanac. The heart divides it into periods. When the sheep-shearing had been forgotten by all others, the squire often looked back to it with longing. It was a boundary which he could never repass, and which shut him out forever from the happy days of his daughters' girlhood,—the days when they had no will but his will, and no pleasures but in his smile and companionship. His son Harry had never been to him what Sophia and Charlotte were. Harry had spent his boyhood in public schools, and, when his education was completed, had defied all the Sandal traditions, and gone into the army. At this time he was with his regiment,—the old Cameronian,— in Edinburgh. And in other points, besides his choice of the military profession, Harry had asserted his will against his father's will. But the squire's daughters gave him nothing but delight. He was proud of their beauty, proud of Charlotte's love of out-door pleasures, proud of Sophia's love of books; and he was immeasurably happy in their affection and obedience.

If Sandal had been really a wise man he would have been content with his good fortune; and like the happy Corinthian have only prayed, "O goddess, let the days of my prosperity continue!" But he had the self-sufficiency and impatience of a man who is without peer in his own small arena. He believed himself to be as capable of ordering his daughters' lives as of directing his sheep "walks," or the change of crops in his valley and upland meadows.

Suddenly it had been revealed to him, that Stephen Latrigg had found his way into a life he thought wholly his own. Until that moment of revelation he had liked Stephen; but he liked him no longer. He felt that Stephen had stolen the privilege he should have asked for, and he deeply resented the position the young man had taken. On the contrary, Stephen had been guilty of no intentional wrong. He had simply grown into an affection too sweet to be spoken of, too uncertain and immature to be subjected to the prudential rules of daily life; yet, had the question been plainly put to him, he would have gone at once to the squire, and said, "I love Charlotte, and I ask for your sanction to my love." He would have felt such an acknowledgment to be the father's most sacred and evident right, and he was thinking of making it at the very hour in which Sandal was feeling bitterly toward him for its omission. And thus the old, old tragedy of mutual misunderstanding works to sorrowful ends.

The night of the sheep-shearing the squire could not sleep. To lay awake and peer into the future through the dark hours was a new experience, and it made him full of restless anxieties. Of course he expected Sophia and Charlotte to

Amelia E. Barr

marry, but not just yet. He had so far persistently postponed the consideration of this subject, and he was angry at Stephen Latrigg for showing him that further delay might be dangerous to his own plans.

"A presumptuous young coxcomb," he muttered. "Does he think that being 'top-shearer' gives him a right to make love to Charlotte Sandal?"

In the morning he wrote the following letter:—

NEPHEW JULIUS SANDAL,—I hear you are at Oxford, and I should think you would wish to make the acquaintance of your nearest relatives. They will be glad to see you at Seat-Sandal during the vacation, if your liking leads you that way. To hear soon from you is the hope of your affectionate uncle,

WILLIAM SANDAL, *of Sandal-Side.*

He finished the autograph with a broad flourish, and handed the paper to his wife. "What do you think of that, Alice? Eh? What?"

There was a short silence, then Mrs. Sandal laid the note upon the table. "I don't think over much of it, William. Good-fortune won't bear hurrying. Can't you wait till events ripen naturally?"

"And have all my plans put out of the way?"

"Are you sure that your plans are the best plans?"

"They will be a bit better than any Charlotte and Stephen Latrigg have made."

"I don't believe they have such a thing as a plan between them. But if you think so, send Charlotte to her aunt Lockerby for a few months. Love is just like fire: it goes out if it hasn't fuel."

"Nay, I want Charlotte here. After our Harry, Julius is the next heir, and I'm set on him marrying one of the girls. If he doesn't like Sophia he may like Charlotte. I have two chances then, and I'm not going to throw one away for Steve Latrigg's liking or loving. Don't you see, Alice? Eh? What?"

"No: I never was one to see beyond the horizon. But if you must have to-morrow in to-day, why then send off your letter. I would let 'well' alone. When change comes to the door, it is time enough to ask it over the threshold. We are very happy now, William, and every happy day is so much certain gain in life."

"That is a woman's way of talking. A man looks for the future."

"And how seldom does he get what he looks for. But I know you, William Sandal. You will take your own way, be it good or bad; and what is more, you will make others take it with you."

"I am inviting my own nephew, Alice. Eh? What?"

"You know nothing about it. There are kin that are not kindred. You are inviting you know not who or what. But,"— and she pushed the letter towards him, with a gesture which seemed to say, "I am not responsible for the consequences."

The squire after a moment's thought accepted them. He went into the yard, humming a strain of "The Bay of Biscay," and gave the letter to a groom, with orders to take it at once to the post-office. Then he called Charlotte from the rose-walk. "The horses are saddled," he said, "and I want you to trot over to Dalton with me."

Mrs. Sandal had gone to her eldest daughter. She was in the habit of seeking Sophia's advice; or, more strictly speaking, she liked to discuss with her the things she had already determined to do. Sophia was sitting in the coolest and prettiest of gowns, working out with elaborate care a pencil drawing of Rydal Mount. She listened to her mother with the utmost respect and attention, and her fine color brightened slightly at the mention of Julius Sandal; but she never neglected once to change an F or an H pencil for a B at the precise stroke the change was necessary.

"And so you see, Sophia, we may have a strange young man in the house for weeks, and where to put him I can't decide. And I wanted to begin the preserving and the raspberry vinegar next week, but your father is as thoughtless as ever was; and I am sure if Julius is like *his* father he'll be no blessing in a house, for I have heard your grandmother speak in such a way of her son Tom."

"I thought uncle Tom was grandmother's favorite."

"I mean of his high temper and fine ways, and his quarrels with his eldest brother Launcelot."

"Oh! What did they quarrel about?"

"A good many things; among the rest, about the Latriggs. There was more than one pretty girl at Up-Hill then, and the young men all knew it. Tom and his mother were always finger and thumb. He was her youngest boy, and she fretted after him all her life."

"And uncle Launcelot, did she not fret for him?"

"Not so much. Launcelot was the eldest, and very set in his own way: she couldn't order him around."

"The eldest? Then father would not have been squire of Sandal-Side if Launcelot had lived?"

"No, indeed. Launcelot's death made a deal of difference to your father and me. Father was very solemn and set about his brother's rights; and even after grandfather died, he didn't like to be called 'squire' until every hope was long gone. But I would as soon have thought of poor Launcie coming back from the dead as of Tom's son visiting here; and it is inconvenient right now, exceedingly so; harvesting coming on, and preserving time, and none of the spare rooms opened since the spring cleaning."

"It is trying for you, mother, but perhaps Julius may not be very much trouble. He'll be with father all the time, and he'll make a change."

"Change! That is just what I dread. Young people are always for change. They are certain that every change must be a gain. Old people know that changes mean loss of some kind or other. After one is forty years old, Sophia, the seasons bring change enough."

"I dare say they do, mother. I don't care much for change, even at my age. Have you told Charlotte?"

"No, I haven't told her yet. I think she is off to Dalton. Father said he was going this morning, and he never would go without her."

Indeed, the squire and his younger daughter were at that

moment cantering down the valley, mid the fresh green of the fields, and the yellow of the ripening wheat, and the hazy purple of mountains holding the whole landscape in their solemn shelter except in front, where the road stretched to the sea, amid low hills overgrown with parsley-fern and stag's-horn-moss. They had not gone very far before they met Stephen Latrigg. He was well mounted and handsomely dressed; and, as he bowed to the squire and Charlotte, his happy face expressed a delight which Sandal in his present mood felt to be offensive. Evidently Steve intended to accompany them as far as their roads were identical; but the squire pointedly drew rein, and by the cool civility of his manner made the young man so sensible of his intrusion, that he had no alternative but to take the hint. He looked at Charlotte with eyes full of tender reproach, and she was too unprepared for such a speedy termination to their meeting to oppose it. So Stephen was galloping at headlong speed in advance, before she realized that he had been virtually refused their company.

"Father, why did you do that?"

"Do what, Charlotte? Eh? What?"

"Send Steve away. I am sure I do not know what to make of you doing such a thing. Poor Steve!"

"Well, then, I had my reason for it. Did you see the way he looked at you? Eh? What?"

"Dear me! A cat may look at a king. Did you send Steve away for a look? You have put me about, father."

"There's looks and other looks, my lass. Cats don't look at kings the way Steve looked at you. Now, then, I want no love-making between you and Steve Latrigg."

"What nonsense! Steve hasn't said a word of love-making, as you call it."

"I thought you had all your woman-senses, Charlotte. Bethink you of the garden walk last night."

"We were talking all the time of the sweetbrier and holly-hocks,—and things like that."

"You might have talked of the days of the week or the multiplication-table: one kind of words was just as good as another. Any thing Steve said last night could have been spelled with four letters."

"Four letters?"

"To be sure. L-o-v-e."

"You used to like Stephen."

"I like all bright, honest, good lads; but when they want to make love to Miss Charlotte Sandal, they think one thing, and I think another. There has been ill-luck with love-making between the Sandals and the Latriggs. My brothers Launcie and Tom quarrelled about one of Barf Latrigg's daughters, and mother lost them both through her. There is no love-line between the two houses, or if there is nothing can make it run straight. Don't you try to, Charlotte; neither the dead nor the living will like it or have it."

He intended then to tell her about Julius Sandal, but a look at her face checked him. He had a wise perception about women; and he reflected that he had very seldom repented of speaking too little to them, but very often repented of speaking too much. So he dropped Stephen, and dropped Julius; and began to talk about the fish in the becks and tarns, and the new breed of sheep he was trying in the lower "walks." Ere long they came into the rich valley of Furness; and he made her notice the difference between it and the vale of Esk and Duddon, with its dreary waste of sullen moss and unfruitful solitudes.

"Those old Cistercian monks that built Furness Abbey knew how to choose a bit of good land, Charlotte. Eh? What?"

"I suppose so. What did they do with it?"

"Let it out."

"I wonder who would want to come here seven hundred years ago."

"You don't know what you are saying, Charlotte. There were great men here then, and great deeds doing. King Stephen kept things very lively; and the Scots were always running over the Border for cattle and sheep, and any thing else they could lay their hands on. And the monks had great flocks, so they rented their lands to companies of four fighting men; and one of the four was to be ready day and night to protect the sheep, and the Scots kept them busy. Eh? What?"

"The Musgraves and Armstrongs and Netherbys, I know," and the cloud passed from her face; and to the clatter of her horse's hoofs, she lilted merrily a stanza of an old border song:—

"The mountain sheep were sweeter,
But the valley sheep were fatter;
We therefore deemed it meeter
To carry off the latter.
We made an expedition;
We met a force, and quelled it;

We took a strong position,
And killed the men who held it."

And the squire, who knew the effort it cost her, fell readily into her mood of forced gayety until the simulated feeling became a real one; and they entered Dalton neck and neck together, after a mile's hard race.

In the mean time the letter which was to summon Fate sped to its destination. When it arrived in Oxford, Julius had left Oxford for London, and it followed him there. He was sitting in his hotel the ensuing night, when it was delivered into his hands; and as it happened, he was in a mood most favorable to its success. He had been down the river on a picnic, had found his company very tedious; and early in the day the climate had shown him what it was capable of, even at mid-summer. As he sat cowering before the smoky fire, the rain plashed in the muddy streets, and dripped mournfully down the dim window-panes. He was wondering what he must do with himself during the long vacation. He was tired of the Continent, he was lonely in England; and the United States had not then become the great playground for earth's weary or curious children.

Many times the idea of seeking out his own relations occurred to him. He had promised his father to do so. But, as a rule, people haven't much enthusiasm about unknown relations; and Julius regarded his promise more in the light of a duty to be performed than as the realization of a pleasure. Still, on that dreary night, in the solitary dulness of his very respectable inn, the Sandals, Lockerbys, and Piersons became three possible sources of interest. While his thoughts were drifting in this direction, the squire's letter was received; and the young man, who was something of a fatalist, accepted it as the solution of a difficulty.

"Sandal turns the new leaf for me," he murmured; "the new leaf in the book of life. I wonder what story will be written in it."

He answered the invitation while the enthusiasm of its reception swayed him, and he promised to follow the letter immediately. The squire received this information on Saturday night, as he was sitting with his wife and daughters. "Your nephew Julius Sandal, from Calcutta, is coming to pay us a visit, Alice," he said; and his air was that of a man who thinks he is communicating a piece of startling intelligence. But the three women had already exchanged every possible idea on the subject, and felt no great interest in its further discussion.

"When is he coming?" asked Mrs. Sandal without enthusiasm; and Sophia supplemented the question by remarking, "I suppose he has nowhere else to go."

"I wouldn't say such things, Sophia; I would not."

"He has been in England some months, father."

"Well, then, he was only waiting till he was asked to come. I'm sure that was a proper thing. If there is any blame between us, it is my fault. I sent him a word of welcome last Wednesday morning, and it is very likely he will be here to-morrow. I'm sure he hasn't let any grass grow under his feet. Eh? What?"

Charlotte looked up quickly. "*Wednesday morning.*" She was quite capable of putting this and that together, and by a momentary mental process she arrived at an exceedingly correct estimate of her father's invitation. Her blue eyes scintillated beneath her dropped lids; and, though she went calmly on tying the feather to the fishing-fly she was making, she said, in a hurried and unsteady voice, "I know he will be disagreeable, and I have made up my mind to dislike him."

Julius Sandal arrived the next morning when the ladies were preparing for church. He had passed the night at Ambleside, and driven over to Sandal in the first cool hours of the day. The squire was walking about the garden, and he saw the carriage enter the park gates. He said nothing to any one, but laid down his pipe, and went to meet it. Then Julius made the first step towards his uncle's affection,—he left the vehicle when they met, and insisted upon walking by his side.

When they reached the house, his valet was attending to the removal of his luggage, and they entered the great hall together. At that moment Mistress Charlotte's remarkable likeness seemed to force itself upon the squire's attention. He was unable to resist the impulse which made him lead his nephew up to it. "Let me introduce you, first of all, to your father's mother. I greet you in her name as well as in my own." As he spoke, the squire lifted his hat, and Julius did the same. It was a sudden, and to both men a quite unexpected, ceremonial; and it gave an air, touching and unusual, to his welcome.

And if that man is an ingrate who does not love his native land, how much more *immediate*, tender, and personal must the feeling be for the *home* of one's own race. That stately lady, who seemed to meet him at the threshold, was only the last of a long, shadowy line, whose hands were stretched out to him, even from the dark, forgotten days in which Loegberg Sandal laid the foundations of it. Julius was sensitive, and full of imagination: he felt his heart beat quick, and his eyes grow dim to the thought; and he loitered up the wide, low steps, feeling very like a man going up the phantom stairway of a dream.

Amelia E. Barr

The squire's cheery voice broke the spell. "We shall be ready for church in a quarter of an hour, Julius; will you remain at home, or go with us?"

"I should like to go with you."

"That's good. It is but a walk through the park: the church is almost at its gates."

When he returned to the hall, the family were waiting for him; Mrs. Sandal and her daughters standing together in a little group, the squire walking leisurely about with his hands crossed behind his back. It would have been to some men a rather trying ordeal to descend the long flight of stairs, with three pairs of ladies' eyes watching him; but Julius knew that he had a striking personal appearance, and that every appointment of his toilet was faultless. He knew also the value of the respectable middle-aged valet following him, and felt that his irreproachable manner of serving his hat and gloves was a satisfactory reflection of his own importance.

It is the women of a family that give the tone and place to it. One glance at his aunt and cousins satisfied Julius. Mrs. Sandal was stately and comely, and had the quiet manners of a high-bred woman. Sophia, in white mull, with a large hat covered with white drooping feathers, and a glimmer of gold at her throat and wrists, was at least picturesque. Of Charlotte, he saw nothing in the first moments of their meeting but a pair of bright blue eyes, and a face as sweet and fresh as if it had been made out of a rose. He took his place between the girls, and the squire and his wife walked behind them. Sophia, being the eldest, took the initiative, talking softly and thoughtfully, as it was proper to do upon a Sunday morning.

The sods under their feet were thick and green; the oaks and sycamores above them had the broad shadows of many centuries. The air was balmy with emanations from the woods and fields, and full of the expanding melody of church-bells travelling from hill to hill. Julius was conscious of every thing; even of the proud, shy girl who walked on his left hand, and whose attitude impressed him as slightly antagonistic. They soon reached the church, a very ancient one, built in the bloody days of the Plantagenets by the two knights whose grim effigies kept guard within the porch. It was dim and still when they entered: the congregation all kneeling at the solemn confession; the clergyman's voice, low and pathetic, intensifying silence to which it only added mortal minors of lament and entreaty. He was a small, spare man, with a face almost as white as the vesture of his holy office. Julius glanced up at him, and for a few minutes forgot all his dreamy philosophies, aggressive free thought, and shallow infidelities. He could not resist the influences around him; and when the people rose, and the organ filled the silence with melody, and a young sweet voice chanted joyfully,—

"O come let us sing unto the Lord: let us heartily rejoice in the strength of our salvation.
Let us come before His presence with thanksgiving: and shew ourselves glad in him with Psalms,"—

he turned round, and looked up to the singer, with a heart beating to every triumphant note. Then he saw it was Charlotte Sandal; and he did not wonder at the hearty way in which the squire joined in the melodious invocation, nor at his happy face, nor at his shining eyes; and he said to himself with a sigh, "That is a Psalm one could sing oftener than once in seven days."

He had not noticed Charlotte much as they went to church: he amended his error as he returned to the "seat." And he thought that the old sylvan goddesses must have been as she was; must have had just the same fresh faces, and bright brown hair; just the same tall, erect forms and light steps; just the same garments of mingled wood-colors and pale green.

The squire had a very complacent feeling. He looked upon Julius as a nephew of his own discovering, and he felt something of a personal pride in all that was excellent in the young man. He watched impatiently for his wife to express her satisfaction, but Mrs. Sandal was not yet sure that she had any good reason to express it.

"Is he not handsome, Alice?"

"Some people would think so, William. I like a face I can read."

"I'm sure it is a long way better to keep yourself to yourself. Say what you will, I am sure he will have plenty of good qualities. Eh? What?"

"For instance, a great deal of money."

"Treat him fair, Alice; treat him fair. You never were one to be unfair, and I don't think you'll begin with my nephew."

"No, I'll never be unfair, not as long as I live; and I'll take up for Julius Sandal as soon as I am half sure he deserves it."

"You can't think what a pleasure it would be to me if he fancied one of our girls. I've planned it this many a long day, Alice."

"Well, then, William, if you have a wish as strong as that, it is something more than a wish, it is a kind of right; and I'll never go against you in any fair matter."

"And though you spoke scornful of money, it is a good thing; and the girl Julius marries will be a rich woman. Eh? What?"

"Perhaps; but it is the happiness and not the riches of her child that is a good mother's reward, and a good father's too. Eh, William?"

"Certainly, Alice, certainly." But his unspoken reflection was, "women are that short sighted, they cannot put up with a small evil to prevent a big one."

He had forgotten that "the wise One" and the "Counsellor" thought one day's joys and sorrows "sufficient" for the heart to bear.

CHAPTER IV

THUS RUNS THE WORLD AWAY

"But we mortals
Planted so lowly, with death to bless us,
Sorrow no longer."

"Our choices are our destiny. Nothing is ours that our choices have not made ours."

Julius Sandal had precisely those superficial excellences which the world is ready to accept at their apparent value; and he had been in so many schools, and imbibed such a variety of opinions, that he had a mental suit for all occasions. "He knows about every thing," said Sandal to the clergyman, at the close of an evening spent together,—an evening in which Julius had been particularly interesting. "Don't you think so, sir?"

The rector looked up at the starry sky, and around the mountain-girdled valley, and answered slowly, "He has a great many ideas, squire; but they are second-hand, and do not fit his intellect."

Charlotte had much the same opinion of the paragon, only

she expressed it in a different way. "He believes in every thing, and he might as well believe in nothing. Confucius and Christ are about the same to him, and he thinks Juggernaut only 'a clumsier spelling of a name which no man spells correctly.'"

"His mind is like a fine mosaic, Charlotte."

"Oh, indeed, Sophia, I don't think so! Mosaics have a design and fit it. The mind of Julius is more like that quilt of a thousand pieces which grandmother patched. There they are, the whole thousand, just bits of color, all sizes and shapes. I would rather have a good square of white Marseilles."

"I don't think you ought to speak in such a way, Charlotte. You can't help seeing how much he admires you."

There was a tone in Sophia's carefully modulated voice which made Charlotte turn, and look at her sister. She was sitting at her embroidery-frame, and apparently counting the stitches in the rose-leaf she was copying; but Charlotte noticed that her hand trembled, and that she was counting at random. In a moment the veil fell from her eyes: she understood that Sophia was in love with Julius, and fearful of her own influence over him. She had been about to leave the room: she returned to the window, and stood at it a few moments, as if considering the assertion.

"I should be very sorry if that were the case, Sophia."

"Why?"

"Because I do not admire Julius in any way. I never could admire him. I don't want to be in debt to him for even one-half hour of sentimental affection."

"You should let him understand that, Charlotte, if it be so."

"He must be very dull if he does not understand."

"When father and you went fishing yesterday, he went with you."

"Why did you not come also? We begged you to do so."

"Because I hate to be hot and untidy, and to get my hands soiled, and my face flushed. That was your condition when you returned home; but all the same, he said you looked like a water-nymph or a wood-nymph."

"I think very little of him for such talk. There is nothing 'nymphy' about me. I should hate myself if there were. I am going to write, and ask Harry to get a furlough for a few weeks. I want to talk sensibly to some one. I am tired of being on the heights or in the depths all the time; and as for poetry, I wish I might never hear words that rhyme again. I've got to feel that way about it, that if I open a book, and see the lines begin with capitals, my first impulse is to tear it to pieces. There, now, you have my opinions, Sophia!"

Sophia laughed softly. "Where are you going? I see you have your bonnet on."

"I am going to Up-Hill. Grandfather Latrigg had a fall yesterday, and that's a bad thing at his age. Father is quite put out about it."

"Is he going with you?"

"He was, but two of the shepherds from Holler Scree have just come for him. There is something wrong with the flocks."

"Julius?"

"He does not know I am going; and if he did, I should tell him plainly he was not wanted either at Up-Hill, or on the way to it. Ducie thinks little of him, and grandfather Latrigg makes his face like a stone wall when Julius talks his finest."

"They don't understand Julius. How can they? Steve is their model, and Steve is not the least like Julius."

"I should think not."

"What do you mean?"

"Never mind. Good-by."

She shut the door with more emphasis than she was aware of, and went to her mother for some cordials and dainties to take with her. As she passed through the hall the squire called her, and she followed his voice into the small parlor which was emphatically "master's room."

"I have had very bad news about the Holler Scree flock, Charlotte, and I must away there to see what can be done. Tell Barf Latrigg it is the sheep, and he will understand: he was always one to put the dumb creatures first. The kindest thing that is in your own heart say it to the dear old man for me; will you, Charlotte?"

"You can trust to me, father."

"Yes, I know I can; for that and more too. And there is more. I feel a bit about Stephen. Happen I was less than kind to him the other day. But I gave you good reasons, Charlotte; and I have such confidence in you, that I said to mother, 'You can send Charlotte. There is nothing underhand about her. She knows my will, and she'll do it.' Eh? What?"

"Yes, father: I'll be square on all four sides with you. But I told you there had been no love-making between me and Steve."

"Steve was doing his best at it. Depend upon it he meant love-making; and I must say I thought you made out to understand him very well. Maybe I was mistaken. Every woman is a new book, and a book by herself; and it isn't likely I can understand them all."

"Stephen is sure to speak to me about your being so queer to him. Had I not better tell the truth?"

"I have a high opinion of that way. Truth may be blamed, but it can't be shamed. However, if he was not making love to you at the shearing, won't you find it a bit difficult to speak your mind? Eh? What?"

"He will understand."

"Ay, I thought so."

"Father, we have never had any secrets, you and me. If I am not to encourage Stephen Latrigg, do you want me to marry Julius Sandal?"

"Well, I never! Such a question! What for?"

"Because, at the very first, I want to tell you that I could not do it—*no way*. I am quite ready to give up my will to your will, and my pleasure to your pleasure. That is my duty; but to marry cousin Julius is a different thing."

"Don't get too far forward, Charlotte. Julius has not said a word to me about marrying you."

"But he is doing his best at it. Depend upon it he means marrying; and I must say I thought you made out to understand him very well. Maybe I was mistaken. Every man is a new book, and a book by himself; and it is not likely I can understand them all."

"Now you are picking up my own words, and throwing them back at me. That isn't right. I don't know whatever to say for myself. Eh? What?"

"Say, 'dear Charlotte,' and 'good-by Charlotte,' and take an easy mind with you to Holler Scree, father. As far as I am concerned, I will never grieve you, and never deceive you,— no, not in the least little thing."

So she left him. Her face was bright with smiles, and her words had even a ring of mirth in them; but below all there was a stubborn weight that she could not throw off, a darkness of spirit that no sunshine could brighten. Since Julius had come into their home, home had never been the same. There was a stranger at the table and in all its sweet, familiar places, and she was sure that to her he always would be a stranger. Something was said or done that put them farther apart every day. She could not understand how any Sandal could be so absolutely out of her love and sympathy. Who has not experienced these invasions of hostile natures? Alien voices, characters fundamentally different, yet bound to them by natural ties which the soul refuses to recognize.

The somberness of her thoughts affected her surroundings very much as rain affects the atmosphere. The hills looked melancholy: she was aware of every stone on the road. Alas! this morning she had begun to grow old, for she felt that she had *a past*,—a past that could never return. Hitherto her life had been to-day and to-morrow, and to-morrow always in the sunshine. Hitherto the thought of Stephen had been blended with something that was to happen. Now she knew she must always be remembering the days that for them would come no more. She found herself reviewing even her former visits to Up-Hill. In them also change had begun. And it is over the young, sorrow triumphs most cruelly. They are so easily wounded, so inapt to resist, so harassed by scruples, so astonished at troubles they cannot comprehend, that their very sensitiveness prepares them for suffering. Very bitter tears are shed before we are twenty years old. At forty we have learned to accept the inevitable, and to feel many things possible which we once declared would break our hearts in two.

There was an air of great depression also at Up-Hill. Ducie was full of apprehension. She said to Charlotte, "When men as old as father fall, they stumble at their own grave; and I can't think what I'll do without father."

"You have Steve."

"Steve is going away. He would have left this morning, but for this fresh trouble. I see you are startled, Charlotte."

"I am that. I heard nothing of it. He moves in a great hurry."

"He always moves that way, does Steve."

"How is grandfather?"

"He has had quite a backening since yesterday night. He has got 'the call,' Charlotte. I've had more than one sign of it. Just before he fell he went into the garden, and brought in with him a sprig of 'Death-come-quickly.' [The plant *Geranium Robertianum*.] 'Father,' I asked, 'whatever made you pull that?' Then he looked so queerly, and answered, 'I didn't pull it, Ducie: I found it on the wall.' He was quite curious, and sent me to ask this one and the other one if they had been in the garden. No one had been there; and, at the long end, he said, 'Make no more talk about it, Ducie. There's *them* that go up and down the fellside that no one sees. *They* lift the latch, and wait not for the open door, the king's command being urgent. I have had a message.' He fell an hour afterwards, Charlotte. He did not think he was much hurt at the time, but he got his death-throw. I know it."

"I should like to speak to him, Ducie. Tell him that Charlotte Sandal wants his blessing."

He was lying on the big oak bed in the best room, waiting for his dismissal in cheerful serenity. "Come here, Charlotte," he said; "stoop down, and let me see you once more. My sight grows dim. I am going away, dear."

"O grandfather! is there any thing I can do for you?"

"Be a good girl. Be good, and do good. Stand true to Steve, —remember,—true to Steve." And he did not seem inclined to talk more.

"He is saving his strength for the squire," said Ducie. "He has a deal to say to him."

"Father hoped to be back this afternoon."

"Though it be the darkening when he gets home, ask him to come at once, Charlotte. Father is waiting for him, and I don't think he will pass the turn of the night."

There were many subtle links of sympathy between Up-Hill and Sandal. Death could not be in one house without casting a shadow in the other. Julius privately thought such a fellow-feeling a little stretched. The Latriggs were on a distinctly lower social footing than the Sandals. Rich they might be; but they were not written among the list of county families, nor had they even married into their ranks. He could not understand why Barf Latrigg's death should be allowed to interfere with life at Seat-Sandal. Yet Mrs. Sandal was at Up-Hill all the afternoon; and, though the squire did not get home until quite the darkening, he went at once, without taking food or rest, to the dying man.

"Why, Barf is very near all the same as my own father," he said. And then, in a lower voice, "and he may see my father before the strike of day. I wouldn't miss Barfs last words for a year of life. I wouldn't that."

It was a lovely night,—warm, and sweet with the scent of August lilies, and the rich aromas of ripening fruit and grain. The great hills and the peaceful valleys lay under the soft radiance of a full moon; and there was not a sound but the gurgle of running water, or the bark of some solitary sheep-dog, watching the folds on the high fells. Sophia and Julius were walking in the garden, both feeling the sensitive suggestiveness of the hour, talking softly together on topics people seldom discuss in the sunshine,—intimations of lost powers, prior existences, immortal life. Julius was learned in the Oriental view of metempsychosis. Sophia could trace the veiled intuition through the highest inspiration of Western thought.

"It whispers in the heart of every shepherd on these hills," she said; "and they interpreted for Mr. Wordsworth the dream of his own soul."

"I know, Sophia. I lifted the book yesterday: your mark was in it." And he recited in a low, intense voice,—

"'Our birth is but a sleep and a forgetting:
The soul that rises with us, our life's star,
Hath had elsewhere its setting,
And cometh from afar:
Not in entire forgetfulness,
And not in utter nakedness,
But trailing clouds of glory do we come
From God, who is our home:'"

"Oh, yes!" answered Sophia, lifting her dark eyes in a real enthusiasm.

"Though inland far we be,
Our souls have sight of that immortal sea
Which brought us hither.'"

And they were both very happy in this luxury of mystical speculation. Eternity was behind as before them. Soft impulses from moon and stars, and from the witching beauty of lonely hills and scented garden-ways, touched within their souls some primal sympathy that drew them close to that unseen boundary dividing spirits from shadow-casting men. It is true they rather felt than understood; but when the soul has faith, what matters comprehension?

In the cold sweetness of the following dawn, the squire returned from Up-Hill. "Barf is gone, Alice," were his first words.

"But all is well, William."

"No doubt of it. I met the rector on the hillside. 'How is Barf?' I asked; and he answered, 'Thank God, he has the mastery!' Then he went on without another word. Barf had lost his sight when I got there; but he knew my voice, and he asked me to lay my face against his face. 'I've done well to

Sandal,—well to Sandal,' he muttered at intervals. 'You'll know it some day, William.' I can't think what he meant. I hope he hasn't left me any money. I could not take it, Alice."

"Was that all?"

"When Steve came in he said something like 'Charlotte,' and he looked hard at me; and then again, 'I've done well by Sandal.' But I was too late. Ducie said he had been very restless about me earlier in the afternoon: he was nearly outside life when I got there. We thought he would speak no more; but about three o'clock this morning he called quite clearly, '*Ducie, the abbot's cross.*' Then Ducie unlocked the oak chest that stands by the bed-side, and took from it an ivory crucifix. She put it in his left hand. With a smile he touched the Christ upon it; and so, clasping the abbot's cross, he died."

"I wonder at that, William. A better Church-of-England man was not in all the dales than Barf Latrigg."

"Ay; but you see, Alice, that cross is older than the Church of England. It was given to the first Latrigg of Up-Hill by the first abbot of Furness. Before the days of Wyckliffe and Latimer, every one of them, babe and hoary-head, died with it in their hands. There are things that go deeper down than creeds, Alice; and the cross with the Saviour on it is one of them. I would like to feel it myself, even when I was past seeing it. I would like to take the step between here and there with it in my hands."

In the cool of the afternoon, Julius and the girls went to Up-Hill. He had a solemn curiousness about death; and both personally and theoretically the transition filled him with vague, momentous ideas, relating to all sides of his conscious being. In every land where he had sojourned, the superstitions and ceremonials that attended it were subjects of interest to him. So he was much touched when he entered the deep, cool porch, and saw the little table at the threshold, covered with a white linen cloth, and holding a plate of evergreens and a handful of salt. And when Sophia and Charlotte each scattered a little salt upon the ground, and broke off a small spray of boxwood, he knew instinctively that they were silently expressing their faith in the preservation of the body, and in the life everlasting; and he imitated them in the simple rite.

Ducie met them with a grave and tender pleasure. "Come, and see the empty soul-case," she said softly; "there is nothing to fear you." And she led them into the chamber where it lay. The great bed was white as a drift of snow. On the dark oak walls, there were branches of laurel and snowberry. The floor was fragrant under the feet, with bits of rosemary, and bruised ears of lavender, and leaves of thyme. The casements were wide open to admit the fresh mountain breeze; and at one of them Steve rested in the carved chair that had been his grandfather's, and was now his own.

The young men did not know each other; but this was neither the time nor the place for social civilities, and they only slightly bowed as their eyes met. Indeed, it seemed wrong to trouble the peaceful silence with mere words of courtesy; but Charlotte gave her hand to Stephen, and with it that candid, loving gaze, which has, from the eyes of the beloved, the miraculous power of turning the water of life into wine. And Charlotte perceived this, and she went home happy in the happiness she had given.

Four days later, Barf Latrigg was buried. In the glory of the August afternoon, the ladies of Seat-Sandal stood with Julius in the shadow of the park gates, and watched the long procession winding slowly down the fells. At first it was accompanied by fitful, varying gusts of solemn melody; but as it drew nearer, the affecting tones of the funeral hymn became more and more distinct and sustained. There were at least three hundred voices thrilling the still, warm air with its pathetic music; and, as they approached the church gates, it blended itself with the heavy tread of those who carried and of those who followed the dead, like a wonderful, triumphant march.

After the funeral was over, the squire went back to Up-Hill to eat the arvel-meal, [Death-feast.] and to hear the will of his old friend read. It was nearly dark when he returned, and he was very glad to find his wife alone. "I have had a few hard hours, Alice," he said wearily; "and I am more bothered about Barfs will than I can tell why."

"I suppose Steve got all."

"Pretty nearly. Barf's married daughters had their portions long ago, but he left each of them three hundred pounds as a good-will token. Ducie got a thousand pounds and her right in Up-Hill as long as she lived. All else was for Steve except—and this bothers me—a box of papers left in Ducie's charge. They are to be given to me at her discretion; and, if not given during her lifetime or my lifetime, the charge remains then between those that come after us. I don't like it, and I can't think what it means. Eh? What?"

"He left you nothing?"

"He left me his staff. He knew better than to leave me money. But I am bothered about that box of papers. What can they refer to? Eh? What?"

"I can make a guess, William. When your brother Tom left home, and went to India, he took money enough with him;

but I'm afraid he got it queerly. At any rate, your father had some big sums to raise. You were at college at the time; and though there was some underhand talk, maybe you never heard it, for no one round Sandal-Side would pass on a word likely to trouble the old squire, or offend Mistress Charlotte. Now, perhaps it was at that time Barf Latrigg 'did well to Sandal.'"

"I think you may be right, Alice. I remember that father was a bit mean with me the last year I was at Oxford. He would have reasons he did not tell me of. One should never judge a father. He is often forced to cut the loaf unevenly for the good of every one."

But this new idea troubled Sandal. He was a man of super-sensitive honor with regard to money matters. If there were really any obligation of that kind between the two houses, he hardly felt grateful to Latrigg for being silent about it. And still more the transfer of these papers vexed him. Ducie might know what he might never know. Steve might have it in his power to trouble Harry when he was at rest with his fore-elders. The subject haunted and worried him; and as worries are never complete worries till they have an individuality, Steve very soon became the personal embodiment of mortifying uncertainty, and wounded *amour propre*. For if Mrs. Sandal's suspicion were true, or even if it were not true, she was not likely to be the only one in Sandal-Side who would construe Latrigg's singular disposition of his papers in the same way. Certainly Squire William did not feel as if the dead man had 'done well to Sandal.'

Stephen was equally annoyed. His grandfather had belonged to a dead century, and retained until the last his almost feudal idea of the bond between his family and the Sandals. But the present squire had stepped outside the shadows of the past, and Stephen was fully abreast of his own times. He understood very well, that, whatever these papers related to, they would be a constant thorn in Sandal's side; and he saw them lying between Charlotte and himself, a barrier unknown, and insurmountable because unknown.

From Ducie he could obtain neither information nor assistance. "Mother," he asked, "do you know what those papers are about?"

"Ratherly."

"When can you tell me?"

"There must be a deal of sorrow before I can tell you."

"Do you want to tell me?"

"If I should dare to want it one minute, I should ask God's pardon the next. When I unlock that box, Steve, there is like to be trouble in Sandal. I think your grandfather would rather the key rusted away."

"Does the squire know any thing about them?"

"Not he."

"If he asks, will you tell him?"

"Not yet. I—hope never."

"I wish they were in the fire."

"Perhaps some day you may put them there. You will have the right when I am gone."

Then Steve silently kissed her, and went into the garden; and

Ducie watched him through the window, and whispered to herself, "It is a bit hard, but it might be harder; and right always gets the over-hand at the long end."

The first interview between the squire and Stephen after Barf Latrigg's funeral was not a pleasanter one than this misunderstanding promised. Sandal was walking on Sandal Scree-top one morning, and met Steve. "Good-morning, Mr. Latrigg," he said; "you are a statesman now, and we must give you your due respect." He did not say it unkindly; but Steve somehow felt the difference between Mr. Latrigg and Squire Sandal as he had never felt it when the greeting had only been, "Good-morning, Steve. How do all at home do?"

Still, he was anxious to keep Sandal's good-will, and he hastened to ask his opinion upon several matters relating to the estate which had just come into his hands. Ordinarily this concession would have been a piece of subtle flattery quite irresistible to the elder man, but just at that time it was the most imprudent thing Steve could have done.

"I had an offer this morning from Squire Methley. He wants to rent the Skelwith 'walk' from me. What do you think of him, sir?"

"As how?"

"As a tenant. I suppose he has money. There are about a thousand sheep on it."

"He lives on the other side of the range, and I know him not; but our sheep have mingled on the mountain for thirty years. I count not after him, and he counts not after me;" and Sandal spoke coldly, like a man defending his own order. "Are you going to rent your 'walks' so soon? Eh? What?"

Amelia E. Barr

"As soon as I can advantageously."

"I bethink me. At the last shearing you were all for spinning and weaving. The Coppice Woods were to make your bobbins; Silver Force was to feed your engines; the little herd lads and lassies to mind your spinning-frames. Well, well, Mr. Latrigg, such doings are not for me to join in! I shall be sorry to see these lovely valleys turned into weaving-shops; but you belong to a new generation, and the young know every thing,—or they think they do."

"And you will soon join the new generation, squire. You were always tolerant and wide awake. I never knew your prejudices beyond reasoning with."

"Mr. Latrigg, leave my prejudices, as you call them, alone. To-day I am not in the humor either to defend them or repent of them."

They talked for some time longer,—talked until the squire felt bored with Steve's plans. The young man kept hoping every moment to say something that would retrieve his previous blunders; but who can please those who are determined not to be pleased? And yet Sandal was annoyed at his own injustice, and then still more annoyed at Steve for causing him to be unjust. Besides which, the young man's eagerness for change, his enthusiasms and ambitions, offended him in a particular way that morning; for he had had an unpleasant letter from his son Harry, who was not eager and enthusiastic and ambitious, but lazy, extravagant, and quite commonplace. Also Charlotte had not cared to come out with him, and the immeasurable self-complacency of his nephew Julius had really quite spoiled his breakfast; and then, below all, there was that disagreeable feeling about the Latriggs.

So Stephen did not conciliate Sandal, and he was himself very much grieved at the squire's evident refusal of his friendly advances. There is no humiliation so bitter as that of a rejected offering. Was it not the failure of Cain's attempted propitiation that kindled the flame of hate and murder in his heart? Steve Latrigg went back to Up-Hill, nursing a feeling of indignation against the man who had so suddenly conceived a dislike to him, and who had dashed, with regrets and doubtful speeches and faint praise, all the plans which at sunrise had seemed so full of hope, and so worthy of success.

The squire was equally annoyed. He could not avoid speaking of the interview, for it irritated him, and was uppermost in his thoughts. He detailed it with a faint air of pitying contempt. "The lad is upset with the money and land he has come into, and the whole place is too small for his greatness." That was what he said, and he knew he was unjust; but the moral atmosphere between Steve and himself had become permeated with distrust and dislike. Unhappy miasmas floated hither and thither in it, and poisoned him. When with Stephen he hardly recognized himself: he did not belong to himself. Sarcasm, contradiction, opposing ideas, took possession of and ruled him by the forces of antipathy, just as others ruled him by the forces of love and attraction.

The days that had been full of peaceful happiness were troubled in all their hours; and yet the sources of trouble were so vague, so blended with what he had called unto himself, that he could not give vent to his unrest and disappointment. His life had had a jar; nothing ran smoothly; and he was almost glad when Julius announced the near termination of his visit. He had begun to feel as if Julius were inimical to him; not consciously so, but in that occult way which makes certain foods and drinks, certain winds and weathers, inimical to certain personalities. His presence seemed to have blighted his happiness, as the north wind blighted his myrtles. "If I could only have let 'well' alone. If I had never written that letter." Many a time a day he said such words to his own heart.

In the mean time, Julius was quite unconscious of his position. He was thoroughly enjoying himself. If others were losing, he was not. He was in love with the fine old hall. The simple, sylvan character of its daily life charmed his poetic instincts. The sweet, hot days on the fells, with a rod in his hand, and Charlotte and the squire for company, were like an idyl. The rainy days in the large, low drawing-room, singing with Sophia, or dreaming and speculating with her on all sorts of mysteries, were, in their way, equally charmful. He liked to walk slowly up and down, and to talk to her softly of things obscure, cryptic, cabalistic. The plashing rain, the moaning wind, made just the monotonous accompaniment that seemed fitting; and the lovely girl, listening, with needle half-drawn, and sensitive, sensuous face lifted to his own, made a situation in which he knew he did himself full justice.

At such times he thought Sophia was surely his natural mate,—'the soul that halved his own,' the one of 'nearer kindred than life hinted of.' At other times he was equally conscious that he loved Charlotte Sandal with an intensity to which his love for Sophia was as water is to wine. But Charlotte's indifference mortified him, and their natures were almost antagonistic to each other. Under such circumstances a great love is often a dangerous one. Very little will turn it into hatred. And Julius had been made to feel more than once the utter superfluity of his existence, as far as Charlotte Sandal was concerned.

Still, he determined not to resign the hope of winning her until he was sure that her indifference was not an affectation. He had read of women who used it as a lure. If it were

Charlotte's special weapon he was quite willing to be brought to submission by it. After all, there was piquancy in the situation; for to most men, love sought and hardly won is far sweeter than love freely given.

Yet of all the women whom he had known, Charlotte Sandal was the least approachable. She was fertile in preventing an opportunity; and if the opportunity came, she was equally fertile in spoiling it. But Julius had patience; and patience is the art and secret of hoping. A woman cannot always be on guard, and he believed in not losing heart, and in waiting. Sooner or later, the happy moment when success would be possible was certain to arrive.

One day in the early part of September, the squire asked his wife for all the house-servants she could spare. "A few more hands will bring home the harvest to-night," he said; "and it would be a great thing to get it in without a drop of rain."

So the men and maids went off to the wheat-fields, as if they were going to a frolic; and there was a happy sense of freedom, with the picnicky dinner, and the general air of things being left to themselves about the house. After an unusually merry lunch, Julius proposed a walk to the harvest-field, and Sophia and Charlotte eagerly agreed to it.

It was a joy to be out of doors under such a sky. The intense, repressing greens of summer were now subdued and shaded. The air was subtle and fragrant. Amber rays shone through the boughs. The hills were clothed in purple. An exquisite, impalpable haze idealized all nature. Right and left the reapers swept their sharp sickles through the ripe wheat. The women went after them, binding the sheaves, and singing among the yellow swaths shrill, wild songs, full of simple modulations.

The squire's field was busy as a fair; and the idle young people sat under the oaks, or walked slowly in the shadow of the hedges, pulling poppies and wild flowers, and realizing all the poetry of a pastoral life, without any of its hard labor or its vulgar cares. Mrs. Sandal had given them a basket with berries and cake and cream in it. They were all young enough to get pleasantly hungry in the open air, all young enough to look upon berries and cake and cream as a distinct addition to happiness. They set out a little feast under the trees, and called the squire to come and taste their dainties.

He was standing, without his coat and vest, on the top of a loaded wain, the very embodiment of a jovial, handsome, country gentleman. The reins were in his hand; he was going to drive home the wealthy wagon; but he stopped and stooped, and Charlotte, standing on tip-toes, handed him a glass of cream. "God love thy bonny face," he said, with a beaming smile, as he handed her back the empty glass. Then off went the great horses with their towering load, treading carefully between the hedges of the narrow lane, and leaving upon the hawthorns many a stray ear for the birds gleaning.

When the squire returned he called to Julius and his daughters, "What idle-backs you are! Come, and bind a sheaf with me." And they rose with a merry laugh, and followed him down the field, working a little, and resting a little; and towards the close of the afternoon, listening to the singing of an old man who had brought his fiddle to the field in order to be ready to play at the squire's "harvest-home." He was a thin, crooked, old man, very spare and ruddy. "Eighty-three years old, young sir," he said to Julius; and then, in a trembling, cracked voice, he quavered out,—

"Says t' auld man to t' auld oak-tree,
Young and lusty was I when I kenned thee:
I was young and lusty, I was fair and clear,

Young and lusty was I, many a long year.
But sair failed is I, sair failed now;
Sair failed is I, since I kenned thou.
Sair failed, honey,
Sair failed now;
Sair failed, honey,
Since I kenned thou."

It was the appeal of tottering age to happy, handsome youth, and Julius could not resist it. With a royal grace he laid a guinea in the old man's open palm, and felt fully rewarded by his look of wonder and delight.

"God give you love and luck, young sir. I am eighty-three now, and sair failed; but I was once twenty-three, and young and lusty as you be. But life is at the fag end with me now. God save us all!" Then, with a meaning look at the two pretty girls watching him, he went slowly off, droning out to a monotonous accompaniment, an old love ballad:—

"Picking of lilies the other day,
Picking of lilies both fresh and gay,
Picking of lilies, red, white, and blue,
Little I thought what love could do."

"'*Little I thought what love could do*,'" Julius repeated; and he sang the doleful refrain over and over, as they strolled back to the oak under which they had had their little feast. Then Sophia, who had a natural love of neatness and order, began to collect the plates and napkins, and arrange them in the basket; and this being done, she looked around for the housemaid in order to put it in her charge. The girl was at the other end of the field, and she went to her.

Charlotte had scarcely perceived what was going on. The old man's singing had made her a little sad. She, too, was thinking of "what love could do." She was standing under the tree, leaning against the great mossy trunk. Her brown hair had fallen loose, her cheeks were flushed, her lips crimson, her whole form a glowing picture of youth in its perfect beauty and freshness. Sophia was out of hearing. Julius stepped close to her. His soul was in his face; he spoke like a man who was no longer master of himself.

"Charlotte, I love you. I love you with all my heart."

She looked at him steadily. Her eyes flashed. She threw downward her hands with a deprecating motion.

"You have no right to say such words to me, Julius. I have done all a woman could do to prevent, them. I have never given you any encouragement. A gentleman does not speak without it."

"I could not help speaking. I love you, Charlotte. Is there any wrong in loving you? If I had any hope of winning you."

"No, no; there is no hope. I do not love you. I never shall love you."

"Unless you have some other lover, Charlotte, I shall dare to hope"—

"I have a lover."

"Oh!"

"And I am frank with you because it is best. I trust you will respect my candor."

He only bowed. Indeed, he found speech impossible. Never before had Charlotte looked so lovely and so desirable to him. He felt her positive rejection very keenly.

"Sophia is coming. Please to forget that this conversation has ever been."

"You are very cruel."

"No. I am truly kind. Sophia, I am tired; let us go home."

So they turned out of the field, and into the lane. But something was gone, and something had come. Sophia felt the change, and she looked curiously at Julius and Charlotte. Charlotte was calmly mingling the poppies and wheat in her hands. Her face revealed nothing. Julius was a little melancholy. "The fairies have left us," he said. "All of a sudden, the revel is over." Then as they walked slowly homeward, he took Sophia's hand, and swayed it gently to and fro to the old fiddler's refrain,—

"'Little I thought what love could do.'"

CHAPTER V

CHARLOTTE

"Oh, how this spring of love resembleth
The uncertain glory of an April day!"

"Hammering and clinking, chattering stony names
Of shale and hornblende, rag and trap and tuff,
Amygdaloid and trachyte."

When Charlotte again went to Up-Hill she found herself walking through a sober realm of leafless trees. The glory of autumn was gone. The hills, with their circular sheep-pens, were now brown and bare; and the plaided shepherds, descending far apart, gave only an air of loneliness to the landscape. She could see the white line of the stony road with a sad distinctness. It was no longer bordered with creeping vines and patches of murmuring bee-bent heather. And the stream-bed also had lost nearly all its sentinel rushes, and the tall brakens from its shaggy slopes were gone. But Silver Beck still ran musically over tracts of tinkling stones; and, through the chilly air, the lustered black cock was crowing for the gray hen in the hollow.

Very soon the atmosphere became full of misty rain; and ere

she reached the house, there was a cold wind, and the nearest cloud was sprinkling the bubbling beck. It was pleasant to see Ducie at the open door ready to welcome her; pleasant to get into the snug houseplace, and watch the great fire leaping up the chimney, and throwing lustres on the carved oak presses and long settles, and on the bright brass and pewter vessels, and the rows of showy chinaware. Very pleasant to draw her chair to the little round table on the hearthstone, and to inhale the fragrance of the infusing tea, and the rich aroma of potted char and spiced bread and freshly-baked cheese-cakes. And still more pleasant to be taken possession of, to have her damp shoes and cloak removed, her chill fingers warmed in a kindly, motherly clasp, and to be made to feel through all her senses that she was indeed "welcome as sun-shining."

With a little shiver of disappointment she noticed that there were only two tea-cups on the table; and the house, when she came to analyze its atmosphere, had in it the perceptible loneliness of the absent master. "Is not Stephen at home?" she asked, as Ducie settled herself comfortably for their meal; "I thought Stephen was at home."

"No, he isn't. He went to Kendal three days ago about his fleeces. Whitney's carpet-works have made him a very good offer. Did not the squire speak of it?"

"No."

"Well he knew all about it. He met Steve, and Steve told him. The squire has been a little queer with us lately, Charlotte. Do you know what the trouble is? I thought I would have you up to tea, and ask you; so when Sandal was up here this morning, I said, 'Let Charlotte come, and have a cup of tea with me, squire, I'd be glad.' And he said, 'When?' And I said, 'This afternoon. I am fair lonely without Steve.'

Amelia E. Barr

And he said, 'I'm agreeable. She'll be glad enough to come.' And I said, 'Thank'ee, squire, I'll be glad enough to see her.' But what *is* the matter, Charlotte? The squire has been in his airs with Steve ever so long."

Then Charlotte's face grew like a flame; and she answered, in a tone of tender sadness, "Father thinks Steve loves me; and he says there is no love-line between our houses, and that, if there were, it is crossed with sorrow, and that neither the living nor the dead will have marriage between Steve and me."

"I thought that was the trouble. I did so. As for the living, he speaks for himself; as for the dead, it is your grandmother Sandal he thinks of. She was a hard, proud woman, Charlotte. Her two daughters rejoiced at their wedding-days, and two out of her three sons she drove away from their home. Your father was on the point of going, when his brother Launcie's death made him the heir. Then she gave him a bit more respect, and for pretty Alice Morecombe's sake he stayed by the old squire. Ten years your mother waited for William Sandal, Charlotte."

"Yes, I know."

"Do you love Steve, Charlotte? I am Steve's mother, dear, and you may speak to me as if you were talking to your own heart. I would never tell Steve either this way or that way for any thing. Steve would not thank me if I did. He is one of them that wants to reach his happiness in his own way, and by his own hand. And I have good reasons for asking you such a question, or I would not ask it; you may be sure I have, that you may."

Charlotte had put down her cup, and she sat with her hands clasped upon her lap, looking down into it. Ducie's question took her by surprise, and she was rather offended by it. For Charlotte Sandal had been taught all the reticences of good society, and for a moment she resented a catechism so direct and personal; but only for a moment. Before Ducie had done speaking, she had remembered that nothing but true kindness could have prompted the inquiry. Ducie was not a curious, tattling, meddlesome woman; Charlotte had never known her to interfere in any one's affairs. She had few visitors, and she made no calls. Year in and year out, Ducie could always be found at home with herself.

"You need not tell me, dear, if you do not know; or if you do not want to tell me."

"I do know, Ducie; and I do not mind telling you in the least. I love Stephen very dearly. I have loved him ever since—I don't know when."

"And you have always had as good and as true as you have given. Steve is fondly heart-grown to you, Charlotte. But we will say no more; and what we have said is dropped into my heart like a stone dropped into deep water."

Then they spoke of the rector, how he was failing a little; and of one of the maids at Seat-Sandal who was to marry the head shepherd at Up-Hill; and at last, when there had been enough of indifferent talk to effectually put Steve out of mind, Ducie asked suddenly, "How is Harry, and is he doing well?"

This was a subject Charlotte was glad to discuss with Ducie. Harry was a great favorite with her, and had been accustomed to run to Up-Hill whenever he was in any boyish scrape. And Harry was *not* doing well. "Father is vexed and troubled about him, Ducie," she answered. "Whenever a letter comes from Harry, it puts every thing wrong in the house. Mother goes away and cries; and Sophia sulks because, she says, 'it is a shame any single one of the family should be allowed to make all the rest uncomfortable.'"

"Harry should never have gone into the army. He hasn't any resisting power, hasn't Harry. And there is nothing but temptation in the army. Dear me, Charlotte! We may well pray not to be led into the way of temptation; for if we once get into it, we are no better off than a fly in a spider's web."

She was filling the two empty cups as she spoke, but she suddenly set down the teapot, and listened a moment. "I hear Steve's footsteps. Sit still, Charlotte. He is opening the door. I knew it was he."

"Mother! mother!"

"Here I am, Steve."

He came in rosy and wet with his climb up the fellside; and, as he kissed his mother, he put out his hand to Charlotte. Then there was the pleasantest stir of care and welcome imaginable; and Steve soon found himself sitting opposite the girl he loved so dearly, taking his cup from her hands, looking into her bright, kind eyes, exchanging with her those charming little courtesies which can be made the vehicles of so much that is not spoken, and that is understood without speech.

But the afternoons were now very short, and the happy meal had to be hastened. The clouds, too, had fallen low; and the rain, as Ducie said, "was plashing and pattering badly." She folded her own blanket-shawl around Charlotte; and as there was no wind, and the road was mostly wide enough for two, Steve could carry an umbrella, and get her safely home before the darkening.

How merrily they went out together into the storm! Steve thought he could hardly have chosen any circumstances that would have pleased him better. It was quite necessary that Charlotte should keep close to his side; it was quite natural that she should lift her face to his in talking; it was equally natural that Steve should bend towards Charlotte, and that, in a moment, without any conscious intention of doing so, he should kiss her.

She trembled and stood still, but she was not angry. "That was very wrong, Steve. I told you at the harvest-home what father said, and what I had promised father. I'll break no squares with father, and you must not make me do so."

"I could not help it, Charlotte, you looked so bewitching."

"Oh, dear! the old, old excuse, 'The woman tempted me,' etc."

"Forgive me, dear Charlotte. I was going to tell you that I had been very fortunate in Kendal, and next week I am going to Bradford to learn all about spinning and weaving and machinery. But what is success without you? If I make every dream come to pass, and have not Charlotte, my heart will keep telling me, night and day, '*All for nothing, all for nothing.*'"

"Do not be so impatient. You are making trouble, and forespeaking disappointment. Before you have learned all about manufacturing, and built your mill, before you are really ready to begin your life's work, many a change may have taken place in Sandal-Side. When Julius comes at Christmas I think he will ask Sophia to marry him, and I think Sophia will accept his offer. That marriage would open the way for our marriage."

"Only partly I fear. I can see that squire Sandal has taken a dislike, and your mother was a little high with me when I saw her last."

"Partly your own fault, sir. Why did you give up the ways of your fathers? The idea of mills and trading in these dales is such a new one."

"But a man must move with his own age, Charlotte. There is no prospect of another Stuart rebellion. I cannot do the queen's service, and get rewarded as old Christopher Sandal did. And I want to go to Parliament, and can't go without money. And I can't make money quick enough by keeping sheep and planting wheat. But manufacturing means money, land, influence, power."

"Father does not see these things as you do, Steve. He sees the peaceful dales invaded by white-faced factory-hands, loud-voiced, quarrelling, disrespectful. All the old landmarks and traditions will disappear; also simple ways of living, calm religion, true friendships. Every good old sentiment will be gauged by money, will finally vanish before money, and what the busy world calls 'improvements.' It makes him fretful, jealous, and unhappy."

"That is just the trouble, Charlotte. When a man has not the spirit of his age, he has all its unhappiness. But my greatest fear is, that you will grow weary of waiting for *our hour*."

"I have told you that I shall not. There is an old proverb which says, 'Trust not the man who promises with an oath.' Is not my simple word, then, the best and the surest hope?"

Then she nestled close to his side, and began to talk of his plans and his journey, and to anticipate the time when he would break ground upon Silver Beck, and build the many-windowed factory that had been his dream ever since he had began to plan his own career. The wind rose, the rain fell in a down-pour before they reached the park-gates; but there was a certain joy in facing the wet breeze, and although they did not loiter, yet neither did they hurry. In both their hearts there was a little fear of the squire, but neither spoke of it. Charlotte would not suppose or suggest any necessity for avoiding him, and Steve was equally sensitive on the subject.

When they arrived at Seat-Sandal the main entrance was closed, and Stephen stood with her on the threshold until a man-servant opened slowly its ponderous panels. There was a bright fire burning in the hall, and lights were in the sconces on the walls. Charlotte asked Steve to come in and rest a while. She tried to avoid showing either fear or hurry, and Steve was conscious of the same effort on his own part; but yet he knew that they both thought it well none of the family were aware of her return, or of his presence. She watched him descend the dripping steps into the darkness, and then went towards the fire. An unusual silence was in the house. She stood upon the hearthstone while the servant rebolted the door, and then asked,—

"Is dinner served, Noel?"

"It be over, Miss Charlotte."

So she went to her own room. It was chilly and dreary. The fire had been allowed to die down, and had only just been replenished. It was smoking also, and the candles on her toilet-table burned dimly in the damp atmosphere. She hurriedly changed her gown, and was going down-stairs, when a movement in Sophia's room arrested her attention. It was very unusual for Sophia to be up-stairs at that hour, and the fact struck her significantly. She knocked at the door, and was told rather irritably to "Come in."

Amelia E. Barr

"Dear me, Sophia! what is the matter? It feels as if there were something wrong in the house."

"I suppose there is something wrong. Father got a letter from Harry by the late post, and he left his dinner untouched; and mother is in her room crying, of course. I do think it is a shame that Harry is allowed to turn the house upside down whenever he feels like it."

"Perhaps he is in trouble."

"He is always in trouble, for he is always busy making trouble. His very amusements mean trouble for all who have the misfortune to have any thing to do with him. Julius told me that no man in the 'Cameronians' had a worse name than Harry Sandal."

"Julius! The idea of Julius talking badly about our Harry, and to you! I wonder you listened to him. It was a shabby thing to do; it was that."

"Julius only repeated what he had heard, and he was very sorry to do so. He felt it to be conscientiously his duty."

"Bah! God save me from such a conscience! If Julius had heard any thing good of Harry, he would have had no conscientious scruples about silence; not he! I dare say Julius would be glad if poor Harry was out of his way."

"Charlotte Sandal, you shall not say such very unladylike, such unchristianlike, things in my room. It is quite easy to see *whose* company you have been in."

"I have been with Ducie. Can you find me a sweeter or better soul?"

"Or a handsomer young man than her son?"

"I mean that also, certainly. Handsome, energetic, enterprising, kind, religious."

"Spare me the balance of your adjectives. We all know that Steve is square on every side, and straight in every corner. Don't be so earnest; you fatigue me to-night. I am on the verge of a nervous headache, and I really think you had better leave me." She turned her chair towards the fire as she spoke, and hardly palliated this act of dismissal by the faint "excuse me," which accompanied it. And Charlotte made no remark, though she left her sister's room, mentally promising herself to keep away from it in the future.

She went next to the parlor. The squire's chair was empty, and on the little stand at its side, the "Gentleman's Magazine" lay uncut. His slippers, usually assumed after dinner, were still warming on the white sheepskin rug before the fire. But the large, handsome face, that always made a sunshiny feeling round the hearth, was absent; and the room had a loneliness that made her heart fear. She waited a few minutes, looking with expectation towards a piece of knitting which was Mrs. Sandal's evening work. But the ivory needles and the colored wools remained uncalled for, and she grew rapidly impatient, and went to her mother's room. Mrs. Sandal was lying upon her couch, exhausted with weeping; and the squire sat holding his head in his hands, the very picture of despondency and sorrow.

"Can I come and speak to you, mother?"

The squire answered, "To be sure you can, Charlotte. We are glad to see you. We are in trouble, my dear."

"Is it Harry, father?"

"Trouble mostly comes that way. Yes, it is Harry. He is in a great strait, and wants five hundred pounds, Charlotte; five hundred pounds, dear, and he wants it at once. Only six weeks ago he wrote in the same way for a hundred and fifty pounds. He is robbing me, robbing his mother, robbing Sophia and you."

"William, I wouldn't give way to temper that road; calling your own son and my son a thief. It's not fair," said Mrs. Sandal, with considerable asperity.

"I must call things by their right names, Alice. I call a cat, a cat; and I call our Harry a thief; for I don't know that forcing money from a father is any better than forcing it from a stranger. It is only using a father's love as a pick-lock instead of an iron tool. That's all the difference, Alice; and I don't think the difference is one that helps Harry's case much. Eh? What?"

"Dear me! it is always money," sighed Charlotte.

"Your father knows very well that Harry must have the money, Charlotte. I think it is cruel of him to make every one ill before he gives what is sure to be given in the end. Sophia has a headache, I dare say, and I am sure I have."

"But I cannot give him this money, Alice. I have not realized on my wool and wheat yet. I cannot coin money. I will not beg or borrow it. I will not mortgage an acre for it."

"And you will let your only son the heir of Sandal-Side, go to jail and disgrace for five hundred pounds. I never heard tell of such cruelty. Never, never, never!"

"You do not know what you are saying, Alice. Tell me how I am to find five hundred pounds. Eh? What?"

"There must be ways. How can a woman tell?"

"Father, have I not got some money of my own?"

"You have the accrued interest on the thousand pounds your grandmother left you. Sophia has the same."

"Is the interest sufficient?"

"You have drawn from it at intervals. I think there is about three hundred pounds to your credit."

"Sophia will have nearly as much. Call her, father. Surely between us we can arrange five hundred pounds. I shall be real glad to help Harry. Young men have so many temptations now, father. Harry is a good sort in the main. Just have a little patience with him. Eh, father?"

And the squire was glad of the pleading voice. Glad for some one to make the excuses he did not think it right to make. Glad to have the little breath of hope that Charlotte's faith in her brother gave him. He stood up, and took her face between his hands and kissed it. Then he sent a servant for Sophia; and after a short delay the young lady appeared, looking pale and exceedingly injured.

"Did you send for me, father?"

"Yes, I did. Come in and sit down. There is something to be done for Harry, and we want your help, Sophia. Eh? What?"

She pushed a chair gently to the table, and sat down languidly. She was really sick, but her air and attitude was that of a person suffering an extremity of physical anguish. The squire looked at her and then at Charlotte with dismay and self-reproach.

"Harry wants five hundred pounds, Sophia."

"I am astonished he does not want five thousand pounds. Father, I would not send him a sovereign of it. Julius told me about his carryings-on."

She could hardly have said any words so favorable to Harry's cause. The squire was on the defensive for his own side in a moment.

"What has Julius to do with it?" he cried. "Sandal-Side is not his property, and please God it never will be. Harry is one kind of a sinner, Julius is another kind of a sinner. God Almighty only knows which kind of sinner is the meaner and worse. The long and the short of it, is this: Harry must have five hundred pounds. Charlotte is willing to give the balance of her interest account, about three hundred pounds, towards it. Will you make up what is lacking, out of your interest money? Eh? What?"

"I do not know why I should be asked to do this, I am sure."

"Only because I have no ready money at present. And because, however bad Harry is, he is your brother. And because he is heir of Sandal, and the honor of the name is worth saving. And because your mother will break her heart if shame comes to Harry. And there are some other reasons too; but if mother, brother, and honor don't seem worth while to you, why, then, Sophia, there is no use wasting words. Eh? What?"

"Let father have what is needed, Sophia. I will pay you back."

"Very well, Charlotte; but I think it is most unjust, most iniquitous, as Julius says"—

"Now, then, don't quote Julius to me. What right had he to be discussing my family matters, or Sandal matters either, I wonder? Eh? What?"

"He is in the family."

"Is he? Very well, then, I am still the head of the family. If he has any advice to offer, he can come to me with it. Eh? What?"

"Father, I am as sick as can be to-night."

"Go thy ways then. Mother and I are both poorly too. Good-night, girls, both." And he turned away with an air of hopeless depression, that was far more pitiful than the loudest complaining.

The sisters went away together, silent, and feeling quite "out" with each other. But Sophia really had a nervous attack, and was shivery and sick with it. By the lighted candle in her hand, Charlotte saw that her very lips were white, and that heavy tears were silently rolling down her wan cheeks. They washed all of Charlotte's anger away; she forgot her resolution not to enter her sister's room again, and at its door she said, "Let me stay with you till you can sleep, Sophia; or I will go, and ask Ann to make you a cup of strong coffee. You are suffering very much."

"Yes, I am suffering; and father knows how I do suffer with these headaches, and that any annoyance brings them on; and yet, if Harry cries out at Edinburgh, every one in Seat-Sandal must be put out of their own way to help him. And I do think it is a shame that our little fortunes are to be crumbled as a kind of spice into his big fortune. If Harry does not know the value of money I do."

"I will pay you back every pound. I really do not care a bit about money. I have all the dress I want. You buy books and music, I do not. I have no use for my money except to make happiness with it; and, after all, that is the best interest I can possibly get."

"Very well. Then, you can pay Harry's debts if it gives you pleasure. I suppose I am a little peculiar on this subject. Last Sunday, when the rector was preaching about the prodigal son, I could not help thinking that the sympathy for the bad young man was too much. I know, if I had been the elder brother, I should have felt precisely as he did. I don't think he ought to be blamed. And it would certainly have been more just and proper for the father to have given the feast and the gifts to the son who never at any time transgressed his commandments. You see, Charlotte, that parable is going on all over the world ever since; going on right here in Seat-Sandal; and I am on the elder brother's side. Harry has given me a headache to-night; and I dare say he is enjoying himself precisely as the Jerusalem prodigal did before the swine husks, when it was the riotous living."

"Have a cup of coffee, Sophy. I'll go down for it. You are just as trembly and excited as you can be."

"Very well; thank you, Charlotte. You always have such a bright, kind face. I am afraid I do not deserve such a good sister."

"Yes, you do deserve all I can help or pleasure you in." And then, when the coffee had been taken, and Sophia lay restless and wide-eyed upon her bed, Charlotte proposed to read to her from any book she desired; an offer involving no small degree of self-denial, for Sophia's books were very rarely interesting, or even intelligible, to her sister. But she lifted the nearest two, Barret's "Maga," and "The Veiled Prophet," and rather dismally asked which it was to be?

"Neither of them, Charlotte. The 'Maga' makes me think, and I know you detest poetry. I got a letter to-night from Agnes Bulteel, and it appears to be about Professor Sedgwick. I was so annoyed at Harry I could not feel any interest in it then; but, if you don't object, I should like to hear you read it now."

"Object? No, indeed. I think a great deal of the old professor. What gay times father and I have had on the Screes with him, and his hammer and leather bags! And, as Agnes writes a large, round hand, and does not fresco her letters, I can read about the professor easily."

RESPECTED MISS SANDAL,—I have such a thing to tell you about Professor Sedgwick and our Joe; hoping that the squire or Miss Charlotte may see him, and let him know that Joe meant no harm at all. One hot forenoon lately, when we were through at home, an old gentlemanly make of a fellow came into our fold, and said, quite natural, that he wanted somebody to go with him on to the fells. We all stopped, and took a good look at him before anybody spoke; but at last father said, middling sharp-like,—he always speaks that way, does father, when we're busy,—

"We've something else to do here than go raking over the fells on a fine day like this with nobody knows who."

He gave father a lile, cheerful bit of a laugh, and said he didn't want to hinder work; but he would give anybody that knew the fells well a matter of five shillings to go with him, and carry his two little bags. And father says to our Joe, "Away with thee! It's a crown more than ever thou was worth at home." So the strange man gave Joe two little leather bags to carry; and Joe thought he was going to make his five shillings middling easy, for he never expected he would find any thing on the fells to put into the bags. But Joe was mistaken. The old gentleman, he said, went louping over wet spots and great stones, and scraffling over crags and screes, till you would have thought he was some kin to a Herdwick sheep.

Charlotte laughed heartily at this point. "It is just the way Sedgwick goes on. He led father and me exactly such a chase one day last June."

"I dare say he did. I remember you looked like it. Go on."

After a while he began looking hard at all the stones and crags he came to; and then he took to breaking lumps off them with a queer little hammer he had with him, and stuffing the bits into the bags that Joe was carrying. He fairly capped Joe then. He couldn't tell what to make of such a customer. At last Joe asked him why ever he came so far up the fell for little bits of stone, when he might get so many down in the dales? He laughed, and went on knapping away with his little hammer, and said he was a jolly-jist.

"Geologist she means, Charlotte."

"Of course; but Agnes spells it 'jolly-jist.'"

"Agnes ought to know better. She waited table frequently, and must have heard the word pronounced. Go on, Charlotte."

He kept on at this feckless work till late in the afternoon, and by that time he had filled both bags full with odd bits of stone. Joe said he hadn't often had a harder darrack after sheep at clipping-time than he had after that old man, carrying his leather bags. But, however, they got back to our house, and mother gave the stranger some bread and milk; and after he had taken it, and talked with father about sheep-farming and such like, he paid Joe his five shillings like a man, and told him he would give him another five shillings if he would bring his bags full of stones down to Skeal-Hill by nine o'clock in the morning.

"Are you sleepy Sophy?"

"Oh, dear, no! Go on."

Next morning Joe took the bags, and started for Skeal-Hill. It was another hot morning; and he hadn't gone far till he began to think that he was as great a fool as the jolly-jist to carry broken stones to Skeal-Hill, when he could find plenty on any road-side close to the place he was going to. So he shook them out of the bags, and stepped on a gay bit lighter without them. When he got near to Skeal-Hill he found old Abraham Atchisson sitting on a stool, breaking stones to mend roads with; and Joe asked him if he could fill his leather bags from his heap. Abraham told Joe to take them that wasn't broken if he wanted stones; so Joe told him how it was, and all about it. The old man was like to tottle off his stool with laughing, and he said, "Joe take good care of thysen'; thou art over sharp to live very long in this world; fill thy bags, and make on with thee."

"Don't you remember old Abraham, Sophy? He built the stone dyke at the lower fold."

"No, I do not remember, I think."

"You are getting sleepy. Shall I stop?"

"No, no; finish the letter."

When Joe got to Skeal-Hill, the jolly-jist had just got his breakfast, and they took Joe into the parlor to him. He laughed all over when Joe went in with the bags, and told him to set them down in a corner, and asked him if he would have some breakfast. Joe had had his porridge, but he said he didn't mind; so he told them to bring in some more coffee and eggs, and ham and toasted bread; and Joe got such a breakfast as isn't common with him, while the old gentleman was getting himself ready to go off in a carriage that was waiting at the door for him. When he came down-stairs he gave Joe another five shillings, and paid for Joe's breakfast, and for what he had eaten himself. Then he told him to put the leather bags beside the driver's feet, and into the carriage he got, and laughed, and nodded, and away he went; and then Joe heard them say he was Professor Sedgwick, a great jolly-jist. And Joe thinks it would be a famous job if father could sell all of the stones on our fell at five shillings a bagful, and a breakfast at odd times. And would it not be so, Miss Sandal? But I'm not easy in my mind about Joe changing the stones; though, as Joe says, one make of stone is about the same as another.

"Sophia, you are sleepy now."

"Yes, a little. You can finish to-morrow."

Then she laid down the simple letter, and sat very still for a little while. Her heart was busy. There is a solitary place that girdles our life into which it is good to enter at the close of every day. There we may sit still with our own soul, and commune with it; and out of its peace pass easily into the shadowy kingdom of sleep, and find a little space of rest prepared. So Charlotte sat in quiet meditation until Sophia was fathoms deep below the tide of life. Sight, speech, feeling, where were they gone? Ah! when the door is closed, and the windows darkened, who can tell what passes in the solemn temple of mortality? Are we unvisited then? Unfriended? Uncounselled?

"Behold!
The solemn spaces of the night are thronged
By bands of tender dreams, that come and go
Over the land and sea; they glide at will
Through all the dim, strange realms of men asleep,
And visit every soul."

CHAPTER VI

THE DAY BEFORE CHRISTMAS

"Still to ourselves in every place consigned.
Our own felicity we make or find."

"Catch, then, oh, catch the transient hour!
Improve each moment as it flies.
Life's a short summer, man a flower;
He dies, alas! how soon he dies!"

There are days which rise sadly, go on without sunshine, and pass into night without one gleam of color. Life, also, has these pallid, monotonous hours. A distrust of all things invades the soul, and physical inertia and mental languor make daily existence a simple weight. It was Christmas-time, but the squire felt none of the elation of the season. He was conscious that the old festal preparations were going on, but there was no response to them in his heart. Julius had arrived, and was helping Sophia to hang the holly and mistletoe. But Sandal knew that his soul shrank from the nephew he had called into his life; knew that the sound of his voice irritated him, that his laugh filled him with resentment, that his very presence in the house seemed to desecrate it, and to slay for him the very idea of home.

He was sitting in the "master's room," wondering how the change had come about. But he found nothing to answer the wonder, because he was looking for some palpable wrong, some distinctive time or cause. He was himself too simple-hearted to reflect that it is seldom a great fault which destroys liking for a person. A great fault can be forgiven. It is small personal offences constantly repeated; little acts of meanness, and, above all, the petty plans and provisions of a selfish nature. Besides which, the soul has often marvellous intuitions, unmasking men and things; premonitions, warnings, intelligences, that it cannot doubt and cannot explain.

Inside the house there was a pleasant air and stir of preparation; the rapid movements of servants, the shutting and opening of doors, the low laughter of gay hearts well contented with the time and the circumstances. Outside, the mesmerizing snow was falling with a soft, silent persistence. The squire looked sadly at the white hills, and the white park, and the branches bending under their load, and the sombre sky, gray upon darker gray.

Last Christmas the girls had relied entirely upon his help. He had found the twine, and driven the nails, and steadied the ladder when Sophia's light form mounted it in order to hang the mistletoe. They had been so happy. The echo of their voices, their snatches of Christmas carols, their laughter and merry badinage, was still in his heart. He remembered the impromptu lunch, which they had enjoyed so much while at work. He could see the mother come smiling in, with constant samples of the Christmas cheer fresh out of the oven. He had printed the verses and mottoes himself, spent all the afternoon over them, and been rather proud of his efforts. Charlotte had said, "they were really beautiful;" even Sophia had admitted that "they looked well among the greens." But to-day he had not been asked to assist in the decorations. True, he had said, in effect, that he did not wish to assist; but, all the same, he felt shut out from his old pre-eminence; and he could not help regarding Julius Sandal as a usurper.

These were drearisome Christmas thoughts and feelings; and they found their climax in a pathetic complaint, "I never thought Charlotte would have given me the go-by. All along she has taken my side, no matter what came up. Oh, my little lass!"

As if in answer to the heart-cry, Charlotte opened the door. She was dressed in furs and tweeds, and she had the squire's big coat and woollen wraps in her hand. Before he could speak, she had reached his chair, and put her arm across his shoulder, and said in her bright, confidential way, "Come, father, let you and me have a bit of pleasure by ourselves: there isn't much comfort in the house to-day."

"You say right, Charlotte; you do so, my dear. Where shall we go? Eh? Where?"

"Wherever you like best. There is no snow to hamper us yet. Some of the servants are down from Up-Hill. Ducie has sent mother a great spice-loaf and a fine Christmas cheese."

"Ducie is a kind woman. I have known Ducie ever since I knew myself. Could we climb the fell-breast, Charlotte? Eh? What?"

"I think we could. Ducie will miss it, if you don't go and wish her 'a merry Christmas.' You never missed grandfather Latrigg. Old friends are best, father."

"They are that. Is Steve at home?"

"He isn't coming home this Christmas. I wasn't planning about Steve, father. Don't think such a thing as that of me."

"I don't, Charlotte. I don't think of Charlotte Sandal and of any thing underhand at the same time. I'm a bit troubled and out of sorts this morning, my dear."

She kissed him affectionately for answer. She not only divined what a trial Julius had become, but she knew also that his heart was troubled in far greater depths than Julius had any power to stir. Harry Sandal was really at the root of every bitter moment. For Harry had not taken the five hundred pounds with the creditable contrite humiliation of the repenting prodigal. It was even yet doubtful whether he would respond to his parents' urgent request to spend Christmas at Seat-Sandal. And when there is one rankling wrong, which we do not like to speak of, it is so natural to relieve the heart by talking a great deal about those wrongs which we are less inclined to disguise and deny.

In the great hall a sudden thought struck the squire; and he stood still, and looked in Charlotte's face. "You are sure that you want to go, my dear? Won't you be missed? Eh? What?"

She clasped his hand tighter, and shook her head very positively. "They don't want me, father. I am in the way."

He did not answer until they had walked some distance; then he asked meaningly, "Has it come to that? Eh? What?"

"Yes, it has come to that."

"I am very glad it isn't you. And I'm nettled at myself for ever showing him a road to slight you, Charlotte."

"If there is any slight between Julius and me, father, I gave it; for he asked me to marry him, and I plainly told him no."

"Hear—you—but. I *am* glad. You refused him? Come, come, that's a bit of pleasure I would have given a matter of five pounds to have known a day or two since. It would have saved me a few good ratings. Eh? What?"

"Why, father! Who has been rating you?"

"Myself, to be sure. You can't think what set-downs I have given William Sandal. Do you mind telling me about that refusal, Charlotte? Eh? What?"

"Not a bit. It was in the harvest-field. He said he loved me, and I told him gentlemen did not talk that way to girls who had never given them the least encouragement; and I said I did not love him, and never, never could love him. I was very firm, father, perhaps a little bit cross; for I did not like the way he spoke. I don't think he admires me at all now."

"I dare be bound he doesn't. 'Firm and a little bit cross.' It wouldn't be a nice five minutes for Julius. He sets a deal of store by himself;" and then, as if he thought it was his duty not to show too much gratification, he added, "I hope you were very civil, Charlotte. A good asker should have a good nay-say. And you refused him? Well, I *am* pleased. Mother never heard tell of it? Eh? What?"

"Oh, no; I have told no one but you. At the long end you always get at my secrets, father."

"We've had a goodish few together,—fishing secrets, and such like; but I must tell mother this one, eh? She *will* go on about it. In the harvest-field, was it? I understand now why he walked himself off a day or two before the set day. And he is all for Sophia now, is he? Well, I shouldn't wonder if

Sophia will 'best' him a little on every side. You *have* given me a turn, Charlotte. I didn't think of a son-in-law yet,—not just yet. Dear me! How life does go on! Ever since the sheep-shearing it has been running away with me. Life is a road on which there is no turning round, Charlotte. Oh, if there only were! If you could just run back to where you made the wrong turning! If you could only undo things that you have done! Eh? What?"

"Not even God can make what has been, not to have been. When a thing is done, if it is only the taking of a walk, the walk is taken to all eternity."

At the word "eternity," they stood on the brow of the hill which they had been climbing, and the squire said it again very solemnly. "Eternity! How dreadful to spend it in repentance which can undo nothing! That is the most awful conception of the word 'eternity.' Eh? What?"

They were silent a moment, then Sandal turned and looked westward. "It is mizzling already, Charlotte; the snow will turn into rain, and we shall have a downpour. Had we not better go home?"

But Charlotte painted in such glowing colors Ducie's fireside, and the pipe, and the cosey, quiet dinner they would be sure to get there, that the squire could not resist the temptation. "For all will be at sixes and sevens at home," he commented, "and no peace for anybody, with greens and carols and what not. Eh? What?"

"And very likely, as it is Christmas Eve, you may be asked to give Sophia away. So a nice dinner, and a quiet smoke, and an hour's nap will help you through to-night." And the thought in each heart, beyond this one, was "Perhaps Harry will be at home."

Amelia E. Barr

Nobody missed the fugitives. Mrs. Sandal was sure Harry would come, and she was busy preparing his room with her own hands. The brightest fire, the gayest greens, the whitest and softest and best of every thing, she chose for Harry's room.

Certainly they were not missed by Julius and Sophia. They were far too much interested in themselves and in their own affairs. From the first hour of his return to Seat-Sandal, Sophia had understood that Julius was her lover, and that the time for his declaration rested in the main with herself. When the Christmas bells were ringing, when the house was bright with light and evergreens, and the very atmosphere full of happiness, she had determined to give him the necessary encouragement. But the clock of Fate cannot be put back. When the moment arrives, the word is spoken or the deed done. Both of them were prepared for the moment, and yet not just then prepared; for Love still holds his great surprise somewhat in reserve.

They were in the drawing-room. The last vase had been filled, the last wreath hung; and Sophia looked at her beautiful hands, marked with the rim of the scissors, and stained with leaves and berries, in a little affected distress. Julius seated himself on the sofa beside her. She trembled, but he looked at her almost triumphantly. Over Sophia's heart he knew his power. With the questioning, unwinking gaze of love his eyes sought hers, and he tenderly spoke her name, "*Sophia.*" She could answer only by her conscious silence.

"My wife! Mine in lives long forgotten."

"O Julius!"

"Always mine; missed in some existences, recovered in

others, but bringing into every life with you my mark of ownership. See here."

Then he lifted her hand, and opening its palm upward, he placed his own in the same attitude beside it. "Look into them both, Sophia, and see how closely our line of fortune is alike. That is something, but behold." And he showed her a singular mark, which had in his own palm its precise counterpart.

"Is it not also in Charlotte's palm? In others?"

"No, indeed. Among all the women on earth, only yours has this facsimile of my own. It is the soul mark upon the body. Every educated Hindoo can trace it; and all will tell you, that, if two individuals have it precisely alike, they are twin souls, and nothing can prevent their union."

"Did they explain it to you, Julius?"

"An Oriental never explains. They apprehend what is too subtle for words. They know best just what they have never been told. Sophia, this hand of yours fits mine. It is the key to it; the interpreter of my fate. Give me my own, darling."

To Charlotte he would never have spoken in such a tone. She would have resented its claim and authority, and perceived that it was likely to be the first encroachment of a tyranny she did not intend to bow to. But Sophia was easily deceived on this ground. She liked the mystical air it gave to the event; the gray sanction of unknown centuries to the love of to-day.

They speculated and supposed, and were supremely happy. The usual lover wanders in the dreams of the future: they sought each other through the phantom visions of the past. And they were so charmed with the occupation, that they quite forgot the exigencies and claims of the present existence until the rattle of wheels, the stamping of feet, and a joyful cry from Mrs. Sandal recalled them to it.

"It is Harry," said Sophia. "I must go to him, Julius."

He held her very firmly. "I am first. Wait a moment. You must promise me once more: 'My life is your life, my love is your love, my will is your will, my interest is your interest; I am your second self.' Will you say this Sophia, as I say it?" And she answered him without a word. Love knows how such speech may be. Even when she had escaped from her lover, she was not very sorry to find that Harry had gone at once to his own room; for he had driven through the approaching storm, and been thoroughly drenched. She was longing for a little solitude to bethink her of the new position in which she found herself; for, though she had a dreamy curiosity about her pre-existences, she had a very active and positive interest in the success and happiness of her present life.

Suddenly she remembered Charlotte, and with the remembrance came the fact that she had not seen her since the early forenoon. But she immediately coupled the circumstance with the absence of the squire, and then she reached the real solution of the position in a moment. "They have gone to Up-Hill, of course. Father always goes the day before Christmas; and Charlotte, no doubt, expected to find Steve at home. I must tell Julius about Charlotte and Steve. Julius will not approve of a young man like Steve in our family, and it ought not to be. I am sure father and mother think so."

At this point in her reflections, she heard Charlotte enter her own room, but she did not go to her. Sophia had a dislike to wet, untidy people, and she was not in any particular flurry to tell her success. Indeed, she was rather inclined to revel for an hour in the sense of it belonging absolutely to Julius and herself. She was not one of those impolitic women, who fancy that they double their happiness by imparting it to others.

She determined to dress with extraordinary care. The occasion warranted it, surely; for it was not only Christmas Eve, it was also her betrothal eve. She put on her richest garment, a handsome gown of dark blue silk and velvet. A spray of mistletoe-berries was in her black hair, and a glittering necklace of fine sapphires enhanced the beauty and whiteness of her exquisite neck and shoulders. She was delighted with the effect of her own brave apparel, and also a little excited with the course events had taken, or she never would have so far forgotten the privileges of her elder birth as to visit Charlotte's room first on such an important personal occasion.

Charlotte was still wrapped in her dressing-gown, lazily musing before the crackling, blazing fire. Her hands were clasped above her head, her feet comfortably extended upon the fender, her eyes closed. She had been a little tired with buffeting the storm; and the hot tea, which Mrs. Sandal had insisted upon as a preventative of cold, had made her, as she told Sophia, "deliciously dozy."

"But dinner will be ready in half an hour, and you have to dress yet, Charlotte. How do I look?"

"You look charming. How bright your eyes are, Sophia! I never saw you look so well. How much Julius will admire you to-night!"

"As to that, Julius always admires me. He says he used to dream about me, even before he saw me."

"Oh, you know that is nonsense! He couldn't do that. I dare say he dreams about you now, though. I should think he would like to."

"You will have to hurry, Charlotte."

"I can dress in ten minutes if I want to."

"I will leave you now." She hesitated a moment at the door, but she could not bring herself to speak of her engagement. She saw that Charlotte was in one of her "no-matter-every-thing-right" moods, and knew she would take the important news without the proper surprise and enthusiasm. In fact, she perceived that Harry's visit occupied her whole mind; for, as she stood a moment or two irresolute as to her own desires, Charlotte talked eagerly of her brother.

"Well, I hope if Harry is of so much importance in your eyes, you will dress decently to meet him. The rector is coming to dinner also."

"I shall wear my blue gown. If I imitate you, I cannot be much out of the way. Heigh-ho! Heigh-ho! I hope Harry will have a pleasant visit. We must do our best, Sophia, to make him happy."

"O Charlotte, if you have nothing to talk about but Harry, Harry, Harry, I am going! I am very fond of Harry, but I don't pretend to be blind to Harry's faults. Remember how many disagreeable hours he has given us lately. And I must say that I think he was very ungrateful about the hundred and eighty pounds I gave him. He never wrote me a line of thanks."

"You did not give it to Harry, you loaned it to me. Be just Sophia. I have paid you fifteen pounds of it back already, and I shall not buy a single new dress until it is all returned. You will not lose a shilling, Sophia."

"How Quixotic you can be! However, it is no use exciting ourselves to-night. One likes to keep the peace at Yule-tide, and so I will bow down to your idol as much as I can conscientiously."

Charlotte made no answer. She had risen hastily, and with rather unnecessary vigor was rattling the ewer and basin, and plashing out the water. Sophia came back into the room, arranged the glass at the proper angle to give her a last comprehensive review of herself; and this being quite satisfactory, she went away with a smiling complacency, and a subdued excitement of manner, which in some peculiar way revealed to Charlotte the real position of affairs between her sister and Julius Sandal.

"She might have told me." She dashed the water over her face at the implied complaint; and it was easy to see, from the impatient way in which she subsequently unbound her hair, and pulled the comb through it, and from the irritability of all her movements, that she felt the omission to be a slight, not only indicating something not quite pleasant in the past, but prefiguring also she knew not what disagreeable feelings for the future.

"It is not Sophia's fault," she muttered; "Julius is to blame for it. I think he really hates me now. He has said to her, 'There is no need to tell Charlotte, specially; it will make her of too much importance. I don't approve of Charlotte in many ways.' Oh, I know you, sir!" and with the thought she pulled the string of her necklace so impatiently that it broke; and the golden beads fell to her feet, and rolled hither and thither about the room.

The incident calmed her. She finished her toilet in haste, and went down-stairs. All the rooms were lighted, and she saw Julius and Sophia pacing up and down the main parlor, hand in hand, so interested in their *sotto voce* conversation as to be quite unconscious that she had stood a moment at the open door for their recognition. So she passed on without troubling them. She heard her mother's happy laugh in the large dining-room, and she guessed from its tone that Harry was with her. Mrs. Sandal was beautifully dressed in black satin, and she held in her hand a handsome silver salver. Evidently she had been about to leave the room with it, when detained by some remark of her son's; for she was half-way between the table and the door, her pretty, kindly face all alight with love and happiness.

Harry was standing on the hearth-rug, facing the room,—a splendidly handsome young fellow in a crimson and yellow uniform. He was in the midst of a hearty laugh, but when he saw Charlotte there was a sudden and wonderful transformation in his face. It grew in a moment much finer, more thoughtful, wistful, human. He sprang forward, took her in his arms, and kissed her. Then he held her from him a little, looked at her again, and kissed her again; and with that last kiss he whispered, "You good sister. You saved me, Charlotte, with that five hundred pounds."

"I would have given it had it been my all, it been fifty times as much, Harry."

There was no need to say another word. Harry and Charlotte understood each other, and Harry turned the conversation upon his cousin.

"This Indian fellow, this Sandal of the Brahminical caste, what is he like, Charley?"

"He does not admire me, Harry; so how can I admire him?"

"Then there must be something wrong with him in the fundamentals; a natural-born inability to admire what is lovely and good."

"You mustn't say such a thing as that, Harry. I am sure that Sophia is engaged to him."

"Does father like him?"

"Not much; but Julius is a Sandal, after all, and"—

"After me, the next heir. Exactly. It shall not be my fault, Charley, if he does not stand a little farther off soon. I can get married too."

"O Harry, if you only would! It is your duty; and there is little Emily Beverley. She is so beautiful and good, and she adores you, Harry."

"Dear little Emmy. I used to love Emmy a long time ago."

"It would make father so happy, and mother and me too. And the Beverleys are related to mother,—and isn't mother sweet. Father was saying"—

At that moment the squire entered the room. His face was a little severe; but the moment his eyes fell upon Charlotte and Harry, every line of sternness was gone like a flash. Harry's arm was round his sister's waist, her head against his shoulder; but in a moment he gently released himself, and went to his father. And in his nineteenth-century way he said what the erring son of old said, "Father, I have not done right lately. I am very sorry."

Amelia E. Barr

"Say no more, Harry, my lad. There shall be no back reckoning between you and me. You have been mixed up with a sight of follies, but you can over-get all that. You take after me in looks. Up-sitting and down-sitting, you are my son. You come of a good kind; you have a kind heart and plenty of dint;[Dint, energy.] now, then, make a fresh start, Harry. Oh, my dear, dear son!" The father's eyes were full of tears, his face shone with love, and he held the young man's hand in a clasp which forgave every thing in the past, and promised everything for the future.

Then Julius and Sophia came in, and there was barely time to introduce the young men before dinner was served. They disliked each other on sight; indeed, the dislike was anterior to sight, and may be said to have commenced when Harry first heard how thoroughly at home Julius had made himself at Seat-Sandal, and when Julius first saw what a desirable estate and fine old "seat" Harry's existence deprived him of. And in half an hour this general aversion began to particularize itself. The slim, suave youth, with his black eyes and soft speech, and small hands and feet, seemed to Harry Sandal in every respect an interloper. The Saxon in this Sandal was lost in the Oriental. The two races were, indeed, distinctly evident in the two men in many ways, but noticeably in their eyes: Harry's being large, blue, and wide open; those of Julius, very black; and in their long, narrow setting and dreamy look, expressing centuries of tranquil contemplation.

But the dinner passed off very pleasantly, more so than family festivals usually pass. After it the lovers went into private session to consider whether they should declare their new relationship during the evening, or wait until Julius could have a private audience with the squire. Sophia was inclined to the first course, because of the presence of the rector. She felt that his blessing on her betrothal would add a religious grace to the event, but Julius was averse to speak on any matter so private to himself before Harry Sandal. He felt that he could neither endure his congratulations nor his dissent; that, in fact, he did not want his opinion on the matter at all. Besides, he had determined to have but one discussion of the affair, and that must include all pertaining to Sophia's rights and her personal fortune.

While they were deciding this momentous question, the rector and Charlotte were singing over the carols for the Christmas service; the squire was smoking and listening; and Harry was talking in a low voice to his mother. But after the rector had gone, it became very difficult to avoid a feeling of *ennui* and restraint, although it was Christmas Eve. Mrs. Sandal soon went into the housekeeper's room to assist in the preparation of the Yule hampers for the families of the men who worked on the estate. Sandal fell into a musing fit, and soon appeared to be dozing; although Charlotte saw that he occasionally opened his eyes, and looked at the whispering lovers, or else shot her a glance full of sympathetic intelligence.

Music has many according charms, and Charlotte tried it, but with small success. Julius and Sophia had a song in their own hearts, and this night they knew no other. Harry loved his sister very dearly, but he was not inclined to "carolling;" and the repression and constraint were soon evident through all the conventional efforts to be "merry." It was the squire who finally hit upon the circumstance which tided over the evening, and sent every one to bed in a ripple of laughter. For, when the piano was closed, he opened his eyes, and said, "Sophia, your mother tells me she has had a very nice Christmas present from the little maid you took such a liking to,—little Agnes Bulteel. It is a carriage hap made of sheepskins white as the snow, and from some new breed of sheep surely; for the wool is longer and silkier than ever I saw."

"Agnes Bulteel!" cried Charlotte. "O Sophia! where are her last letters? I am sure father would like to hear about Joe and the jolly-jist."

"Joe Bulteel is no fool," said the squire warmly. "It is the way around here to laugh a bit at Joe; but Joe aims to do right, and he is a very spirity lad. What are you and Sophia laughing at? Eh? What?"

"Get the letters, Sophia. Julius and Harry will enjoy them I know. Harry must remember Joe Bulteel."

"Certainly. Joe has carried my line and creel many a day. Trout couldn't fool Joe. He was the one to find plovers' eggs, and to spot a blaeberry patch. Joe has some senses ordinary people do not have, I think. I should like to hear about Joe and the *what*?"

"The jolly-jist,—Professor Sedgwick really. Joe has been on the fells with the professor."

So they drew around the fire, and Sophia went for the letters. She was a good reader, and could give the county peculiarities with all their quaint variations of mood and temper and accent. She was quite aware that the reading would exhibit her in an entirely new *role* to Julius, and she entered upon the task with all the confidence and enthusiasm which insured the entertainment. And as both Professor Sedgwick and Joe Bulteel were well known to the squire and Harry, they entered into the joke also with all their hearts; and one peal of laughter followed another, as the squire's comments made many a distinct addition to the unconscious humor of the letters.

At that point of the story where Joe had triumphantly pocketed his last five shillings, and gone home reflecting on what a "famous job it would be to sell all the stones on their fell at five shillings a little bagful," Mrs. Sandal entered. A servant followed with spiced wine and dainty bits of cake and pastry; and then, after a merry interval of comment and refreshment, Sophia resumed the narrative.

All this happened at the end of May, Miss Sandal; and one day last August father went down Lorton way, and it was gayly late when he got home. As he was sitting on his own side the fire, trying to loose the buttons of his spats, he said to Joe, "I called at Skeal-Hill on my road home." Mother was knitting at her side of the hearth. She hadn't opened her mouth since father came home; nay, she hadn't so much as looked at him after the one hard glower that she gave him at first; but when he said he'd been at Skeal-Hill, she gave a grunt, and said, as if she spoke to nobody but herself, "Ay, a blind body might see that."—"I was speaking to Joe," said father. "Joe," said he again, "I was at Skeal-Hill,"—mother gave another grunt then,—"and they told me that thy old friend the jolly-jist is back again. I think thou had better step down, and see if he wants to buy any more broken stones; old Abraham has a fine heap or two lying aside Kirgat." Joe thought he had done many a dafter thing than take father at his word, whether he meant it or not; and so thought, so done, for next morning he took himself off to Skeal-Hill.

When he got there, and asked if the jolly-jist was stirring yet, one servant snorted, and another grunted, till Joe got rather maddish; but at last one of them skipjacks of fellows, that wear a little jacket like a lass's bedgown, said he would see. He came back laughing, and said, "Come this way, Joe." Well, our Joe followed him till he stopped before a room door; and he gave a little knock, and then opened it, and says he, "Joe, sir." Joe wasn't going to stand that; and he said, "'Joe, sir,' he'll ken its 'Joe, sir,' as soon as he sees the face of me. And get out with thy 'Joe, sir,' or I'll make thee laugh at the wrong side of that ugly face of thine." With that the fellow skipped out of our Joe's way gayly sharp, and Joe stepped quietly into the room.

There the little old gentleman was sitting at a table writing,—gray hair, spectacles, white neck-cloth, black clothes,—just as if he had never either doffed or donned himself since he went away. But before Joe could put out his hand, or say a civil word to him, he glinted up at Joe through his spectacles very fierce like, and grunted out something about wondering how Joe durst show his face again. Well, that put the cap on all for poor Joe. He had thought over what father said, and *how* he said it, on his road down till he found himself getting rather mad about it; and the way they all snorted and laughed when he came to Skeal-Hill made him madder; and that bedgown fellow, with his "Joe, sir," made him madder than ever; but when the old jolly-jist—that he thought would be so fain to see him, if it was only for the sake of their sprogue on the fells together—when he wondered "how Joe durst show his face there," it set Joe rantin' mad, and he *did* make a burst.

At this point the squire was laughing so noisily that Sophia had to stop; and his hearty *ha, ha, ha!* was so contagious, that Harry and Julius and Charlotte, and even Mrs. Sandal, echoed it in a variety of merry peals. Sophia was calmer. She sat by the lamp, pleasantly conscious of the amusement she was giving; and, considering that she had already laughed the circumstance out in her room, quite as well entertained as any of the party. In a few minutes the squire recovered himself. "Let us have the rest now, Sophia. I'd have given a gold guinea to have heard Joe's 'burst.'"

"Show my face?" said Joe; "and what should I show, then? If it comes to showing faces, I've a better face to show than ever belonged to one of your breed, if the rest of them are aught like the sample they have sent us. But if you must know," said Joe, "I come of a stock that never would be frightened to show their face to a king, let alone an old noodles that calls himself a jolly-jist. And I defy the face of clay," said Joe, "to show that any of us ever did aught he need to be ashamed of, wherever we show our faces. Dare to show my face, eh?" said Joe again, "My song! but this is a bonnie welcome to give a fellow that has come so far to see you such a hot morning." Joe said a deal more of the same make; and all the time he was saying it, the old man laid himself back in his great chair, and kept twiddling his thumbs, and glancing up at Joe with a half-smirk on his face, as if he had got something very funny before him.

"Joe is like all these shepherd lads," said the squire, "as independent as never was. They are a manly race, but the Bulteels all come of a good kind."

Julius laughed scornfully, but the squire took him up very short. "You need not laugh, nephew. It is as I say. The Bulteels are as good stock as the Sandals; a fine old family, and, like the Sandals, at home here when the Conqueror came. Joe would do the right thing I'll be bound. Let us hear if he didn't, Sophia."

After a while Joe stopped, for he had run himself very near short of wind; and he began rather to think shame of shouting and bellering so at an old man, and him as whisht as a trout through it all. And when Joe pulled in, he only said, as quietly as ever was, that Joe was a "natural curiosity."

Joe didn't know very well what this meant; but he thought it was sauce, and it had like to have set him off again; but he beat himself down as well as he could, and he said, "Have you any thing against me? If you have, speak it out like a man; and don't sit there twiddling your thumbs, and calling folks out of their names in this road." Then it came out plain enough. All this ill-nature, Miss Sandal, was just because poor Joe hadn't brought him the same stones as he had gathered on the fells; and he said that changing them was either a very dirty trick, or a very clumsy joke.

"Trick," said Joe. "*Joke*, did you say? It was ratherly past a joke to expect me to carry a load of broken stones all the way here, when there was plenty on the spot. I'm not such a fool as you've taken me for," said Joe. The jolly-jist took off his spectacles, and glowered at Joe without them. Then he put them on again, and glowered at Joe with them; and then he laughed, and asked Joe, if he thought there could be no difference in stones. "Why!" answered Joe, "you hardly have the face to tell me that one bag of stones isn't as good as another bag of stones; and surely to man you'll never be so conceited as to say that you can break stones better than old Abraham Atchisson, who breaks them for his bread, and breaks them all day long and every day."

With that the old man laughed again, and told Joe to sit down; and then he asked him what he thought made him take so much trouble seeking bits of stone on the fells, if he could get what he wanted on the road-side. "Well," Joe said, "if I must tell you the truth, I thought you were rather soft in the head; but it made no matter what I thought, so long as you paid me so well for going with you." As Joe said this, it came into his head that it was better to flatter a fool than to fight him; and after all, that there might be something in the old man liking stones of his own breaking better than those of other folks' breaking. We all think the most of what we have had a hand in ourselves, don't we Miss Sandal? It's nothing but natural. And as soon as this run, through Joe's head, he found himself getting middling sorry for the old man; and he said, "What will you give me to get you your own bits of stones back again?"

He cocked up his ears at that, and asked if his "speciments," as he called them, were safe. "Ay," said Joe, "they are safe enough. Nobody hereabout thinks a little lot of stones worth meddling with, so long as they don't lie in their road." With that the jolly-jist jumped up, and said Joe must have something to eat and drink. Then Joe thought to himself, "Come, come, we are getting back to our own menseful way again." But he would not stir a peg till he heard what he was to have for getting the stones again; for Joe knew he would never hear the last of it, if he came home empty-handed. They made it all right very soon, however; and the old man went up-stairs, and brought down the two leather bags, and gave them to Joe to carry, as if nothing had happened; and off they started, very like as they did before.

The Skeal-Hill folk all gathered together about the door to look after them, as if they had been a show; but they neither of them minded for that, but walked away as thick as inkle-weavers till they got to the foot of our great meadow, where the stones were all lying just as Joe had turned them out of the bags, only rather grown over with grass. And as Joe picked them up one by one, and handed them to the old jolly-jist, it did Joe's heart good to see how pleased he looked. He wiped them on his coat-cuff, and wet them, and glowered at them through his spectacles, as if they were something good to eat, and he was very hungry; and then he packed them away into the bags till they were both chock full again.

Well, the bargain was, that Joe should carry them back to Skeal-Hill; so back they put, the jolly-jist watching his bags all the way, as if they were full of golden guineas, and our Joe a thief. When they got there, he made Joe take them right into the parlor; and the first thing he did was to call for some red wax and a light, and he clapped a great splatch of a seal on either bag; and then he looked at Joe, and gave a little grunt of a laugh, and a smartish wag of the head, as much as to say, "Do it again, Joe, if you can." But after that he said, "Here, Joe, is five shillings for restoring my speciments, and here is another five shillings for showing me a speciment of human nature that I did not believe in until this day." [This story is told of Professor Sedgwick in broad *patois* by Alexander Craig Gibson, F.S.A.]

"That is good," cried the squire, clapping his knee emphatically. "It was like the professor, and it was like Joe Bulteel. The story does them both credit. I am glad I heard it. Alice, fill our glasses again." Then he stood up, and looked around with a smile.

"God's blessing on this house, and on all beneath its roof-tree!

"Wife and children, a merry Christmas to you!

"Friends and serving hands, a merry Christmas to you!"

CHAPTER VII

WOOING AND WEDDING

"She was made for him,—a special providence in his behalf."

"Like to like,—and yet love may be dear bought."

"In time comes she whom Fate sends."

Until after Twelfth Night the Christmas festivities were continued; but if the truth had been admitted, the cumbrous ceremonials, the excessive eating and visiting, would have been pronounced by every one very tiresome. Julius found it particularly so, for the festival had no roots in his boyhood's heart; and he did not include it in his dreams of pre-existence.

"It is such semblance of good fellowship, such a wearisome pretence of good wishes that mean nothing," he said one day. "What value is there in such talk?"

"Well," answered the squire, "it isn't a bad thing for some of us to feel obliged once in a twelve months to be good-natured, and give our neighbors a kind wish. There are them that never do it except at Christmas. Eh? What?"

"Such wishes mean nothing."

"Nay, now, there is no need to think that kind words are false words. There is a deal of good sometimes in a mouthful of words. Eh? What?"

"And yet, sir, as the queen of the crocodiles remarked, 'Words mend none of the eggs that are broken.'"

"I know nothing about the queen of the crocodiles. But if you don't believe in words, Julius, it is quite allowable at Christmas time to put your good words into any substantial form you like. Nobody will doubt a good wish that is father to a handsome gift; so, if you don't believe in good words, you have a very reliable substitute in good deeds. I saw how you looked when I said 'A merry Christmas' to old Simon Gills, and you had to say the words after me. Very well; send old Simon a new plaid or a pound of tobacco, and he'll believe in your wish, and you'll believe in yourself. Eh? What?"

The days were full of such strained conversations on various topics. Harry could say nothing which Julius did not politely challenge by some doubtful inquiry. Julius felt in every word and action of Harry's the authority of the heir, and the forbearance of a host tolerant to a guest. He complained bitterly to Sophia of the position in which he was constantly put. "Your father and brother have been examining timber, and looking at the out-houses this morning, and I understand they were discussing the building of a conservatory for Charlotte; but I was left out of the conversation entirely. Is it fair, Sophia? You and I are the next heirs, and just as likely to inherit as Harry. More so, I may say, for a soldier's life is already sold, and Harry is reckless and dissipated as well. I think I ought to have been consulted. I should not be in favor of thinning the timber. I dare say it is done to pay Harry's bills; and thus, you see, it may really be we who are made to suffer. I don't think your father likes our marriage, dear one."

"But he gave his consent, beloved."

"I was very dissatisfied with his way of doing it. He might as well have said, 'If it has to be, it has to be; and there is no use fretting about it.' I may be wrong, but that is the impression his consent left on my mind. And he was quite unreasonable when I alluded to money matters. I would not have believed that your father was capable of being so disagreeably haughty. Of course, I expected him to say something about our rights, failing Harry's, and he treated them as if they did not exist. Even when I introduced them in the most delicate way, he was what I call downright rude. 'Julius,' he said, 'I will not discuss any future that pre-supposes Harry's death.'"

"Father's sun rises and sets in Harry, and it was like him to speak that way; he meant nothing against us. Father would always do right. What I feel most is the refusal to give us our own apartments in Seat-Sandal. We do not want to live here all the time, but we ought to be able to feel that we have a certain home here."

"Yes, indeed. It is very important in my eyes to keep a footing in the house. Possession is a kind of right. But never mind, Sophia. I have always had an impression that this was my home. The first moment I crossed the threshold I felt it. All its rooms were familiar to me. People do not have such presentiments for nothing."

There is a class of lovers who find their supremest pleasure in isolating themselves; who consider their own affairs an oasis of delight, and make it desert all around them. Julius and Sophia belonged to it. They really enjoyed the idea that they were being badly used. They talked over the squire's injustice, Mrs. Sandal's indifference to every one but Harry, and Charlotte's envy, until they had persuaded themselves that they were the only respectable and intelligent members of the family. Naturally Sophia's nature deteriorated under this isolating process. She grew secretive and suspicious. Her love-affairs assumed a proportion which put her in false relations to all the rest of the world.

It was unfortunate that they had come to a crisis during Harry's visit, for of course Harry occupied a large share of every one's interest. The squire took the opportunity to talk over the affairs of the estate with him, and this was not a kind of conversation they felt inclined to make general. It took them long solitary walks to the different "folds," and several times as far as Kendal together. "Am I one of the family, or am I not?" Julius would ask Sophia on such occasions; and then the discussion of this question separated them from it, sometimes for hours at a time.

Mrs. Sandal hardly perceived the growth of this domestic antagonism. When Harry was at Seat-Sandal, she lived and moved and had her being in Harry. His food and drink, and the multitude of his small comforts; his friends and amusements; the renovation of his linen and hosiery; his hopes and fears, and his promotion or marriage, were enough to fill the mother's heart. She was by no means oblivious of Sophia's new interests, she only thought that they could be put aside until Harry's short visit was over; and Charlotte's sympathies were also with Harry. "Julius and Sophia do not want them, mother," she said, "they are sufficient unto themselves. If I enter a room pre-occupied by them, Sophia sits silent over her work, with a look of injury on her face; and Julius walks about, and kicks the stools out of his way, and simply 'looks' me out of their presence."

After such an expulsion one morning, she put on her bonnet and mantle, and went into the park. She was hot and trembling with anger, and her eyes were misty with tears. In the main walk she met Harry. He was smoking, and pacing slowly up and down under the bare branches of the oaks. For a moment he also seemed annoyed at her intrusion on his solitude; but the next one he had tucked her arm through his own, and was looking with brotherly sympathy into her flushed and troubled face. This morning Charlotte felt it to be a great comfort to complain to him, to even cry a little over the breaking of the family bond, and the loss of her sister's affection.

"I have always been so proud of Sophia, always given up to her in every thing. When grandmother showed me the sapphire necklace, and said she was going to leave it to me because she loved me best, I begged her not to slight Sophia in such a way as that,—Sophia being the elder, you know, Harry. I cried about it until she was almost angry with me. Julius offered his hand to me first; and though I claim no merit for giving up what I do not want, yet, all the same, if I had wanted him I should have refused, because I saw that Sophia had set her heart upon him. I should indeed, Harry."

"I believe you would, Charlotte."

"And somehow Julius manages to give me the feeling that I am only in Seat-Sandal on his tolerance. Many a time a day I have to tell myself that father is still alive, and that I have a right in my own home. I do not know how he manages to make me feel so."

"In the same way that he conveys to me the impression that I shall never be squire of Sandal-Side. He has doomed me to death in his own mind; and I believe if I had to live with him, I should feel constrained to go and shoot myself."

"I would come home, and get married, Harry. There will be room enough and welcome enough for your wife in Seat-Sandal, especially if she be Emily."

"She will not be Emily; for I love some one else far away better,—millions of times better than I love Emily."

"I am so glad, Harry. Have you told father?"

"Not yet. I do not think he will be glad, Charlotte."

"But why?"

"There are many reasons."

"Such as?"

"She is poor."

"Oh! that is bad, Harry; because I know that we are not rich. But she is not your inferior? I mean she is not uneducated or unladylike?"

"She is highly educated, and in all England there is not a more perfect lady."

"Then I can see no reason to think father will not be pleased. I am sure, Harry, that I shall love your wife. Oh, yes! I shall love her very dearly."

Then Harry pressed her arm close to his side, and looked lovingly down into her bright, earnest face. There was no need of speech. In a glance their souls touched each other.

"And so he asked you first, eh, Charley?"

"Yes."

"And you would not have him? What for Charley?"

"I did not like Julius, and I did like some one else."

"Oh! Oh! Who is the some one else?"

"Guess, Harry. He is very like you, very: fair and tall, with clear, candid, happy blue eyes; and brown hair curling close over his head. In the folds and in the fields he is a master. His heart is gentle to all, and full of love for me. He has spirit, dint, [Dint, energy.] ambition, enterprise; and can work twenty hours out of the twenty-four to carry out his own plans. He is a right good fellow, Harry."

"A North-country man?"

"Certainly. Do you think I would marry a stranger?"

"Cumberland born?"

"Who else?"

"Then it is Steve Latrigg, eh? Well, Charley, you might go farther, and fare worse. I don't think he is worthy of you."

"Oh, but I do!"

"Very few men are worthy of you."

"Only Steve. I want you to like Steve. Harry."

"Certainly. Seat-Sandal folks and Up-Hill folks are always thick friends. And Steve and I were boy chums. He is a fine fellow, and no mistake. I am glad he is to be my brother. I asked mother about him; and she said he was in Yorkshire, learning how to spin and weave wool—a queer thing, Charley."

"Not at all. He may just as well spin his own fleeces as sell them to Yorkshiremen to spin." Then they talked awhile of Stephen's plans, and Harry appeared to be much impressed with them. "It is a pity father does not join him, Charley," he said. "Every one is doing something of the kind now. Land and sheep do not make money fast enough for the wants of our present life. The income of the estate is no larger than it was in grandfather's time; but the expenses are much greater, although we do not keep up the same extravagant style. I need money, too, need it very much; but I see plainly that father has none to spare. Julius will press him very close."

"What has Julius to do with father's money?"

"Father must, in honor, pay Sophia's portion. Unfortunately, when the fellow was here last, father told him that he had put away from the estate one hundred pounds a year for each of his girls. Under this promise, Sophia's right with interest will be near three thousand pounds, exclusive of her share in the money grandmother left you. I am sorry to say that I have had something to do with making it hard for father to meet these obligations. And Julius wants the money paid at the marriage. Father, too, feels very much as I feel, and would rather throw it into the sea than give it to him; only *noblesse oblige*."

The subject evidently irritated Harry beyond endurance, and he suddenly changed it by taking from his pocket an ivory miniature. He gave it to Charlotte, and watched her face with a glow of pleasant expectation. "Why, Harry!" she cried, "does so lovely a woman really exist?"

He nodded happily, and answered in a voice full of emotion, "And she loves me."

"It is the countenance of an angel."

"And she loves me. I am not worthy to touch the hem of her garment, Charley, but she loves me." Then Charlotte lifted the pictured face to her lips. Their confidence was complete; and they did not think it necessary to talk it over, or to exact promises of secrecy from each other.

The next day Harry returned to his regiment, and Sophia's affairs began to receive the attention which their important crisis demanded. In those days it was customary for girls to make their own wedding outfit, and there was no sewing-machine to help them. "Mine is the first marriage in the family," Sophia said, "and I think there ought to be a great deal of interest felt in it." And there was. Grandmother Sandal's awmries were opened for old laces and fine cambric, and petticoats and spencers of silks wonderful in quality and color, and guiltless of any admixture of less precious material. There were whole sets of many garments to make, and tucking and frilling and stitching were then slow processes. Agnes Bulteel came to assist; but the work promised to be so tedious, that the marriage-day was postponed until July.

In the mean time, Julius spent his time between Oxford and Sandal-Side. Every visit was distinguished by some rich or rare gift to his bride, and he always felt a pleasure in assuring himself that Charlotte was consumed with envy and regret. He was very much in love with Sophia, and quite glad she was going to marry him; and yet he dearly liked to think that he made Charlotte sorry for her rejection of his love, and wistfully anxious for the rings and bracelets that were the portion of his betrothed. Sophia soon found out that this idea

Amelia E. Barr

flattered and pleased him, and it gave her neither shame nor regret to indorse it. She loved no one but Julius, and she made a kind of merit in giving up every one for him. The sentiment sounded rather well; but it was really an intense selfishness, wearing the mask of unselfishness. She did not reflect that the daily love and duty due to others cannot be sinlessly withheld, or given to some object of our own particular choice, or that such a selfish idolatry is a domestic crime.

It was a very unhappy time to Charlotte. Her mother was weary with many unusual cares, her father more silent and depressed than she had ever before seen him. The sunny serenity of her happy home was disturbed by a multitude of new elements, for an atmosphere of constant expectation gave a restless tone to its usual placid routine. And through all and below all, there was that feeling of money perplexity, which, where it exists, is no more to be hid than the subtle odor of musk, present though unseen.

This year the white winter appeared to Charlotte interminable in length. The days in which it was impossible to go out, full of Sophia's sewing and little worries and ostentations; the windy, tempestuous nights, that swept the gathering drifts away; the cloudless moonlight nights, full of that awful, breathless quiet that broods in land-locked dales,—all of them, and all of Nature's moods, had become inexpressibly, monotonously wearisome before the change came. But one morning at the end of March, there was a great west wind charged with heavy rains, and in a few hours the snow on all the fells had been turned into rushing floods, that came roaring down from every side into the valley.

"'Oh, wind!
If winter comes, can spring be far behind?'"

quoted Charlotte, as she stood watching the white cascades.

"It will be cuckoo time directly my dear; and the lambs will be bleating on the fells, and the yellow primroses blowing under all the hedges. I want to see the swallows take the storm on their wings badly this year. Eh? What, Charlotte?"

"So do I, father. I never was so tired of the house before."

"There's a bit of a difference lately, I think. Eh? What?"

Charlotte looked at him; there was no need to speak. They both understood and felt the full misery of household changes that are not entirely happy ones; changes that bring unfaithfulness and ingratitude on one side, and resentful, wounded love on the other. And the worst of it all was, that it might have been so different. Why had the lovers set themselves apart from the family, had secrets and consultations and interests they refused to share? How had it happened that Sophia had come to consider her welfare as apart from, and in opposition to, that of the general welfare of Seat-Sandal? And when this feeling existed, it seemed unjust to Charlotte that they should still expect the whole house and household to be kept in turmoil for the furtherance of their plans, and that every one should be made to contribute to their happiness.

"After all, maybe it is a bit natural," said the squire with a sad air of apology. "I have noticed even the robins get angry if you watch them building their nests."

"But they, at least, build their own nest, father. The cock-robin does not go to his parents, and the hen robin to her parents, and say, 'Give us all the straw you can, and put it down at the foot of our tree; but don't dare to peep into the branches, or offer us any suggestions about the nest, or expect to have an opinion about our housekeeping.' Selfishness spoils every thing, father. I think if a rose could be selfish it would be hideous."

"I don't think a lover would make my Charlotte forget her father and mother, and feel contempt for her home, and all in and about it that she does not want for herself. Why, a stranger would think that Sophia was never loved by any human heart before! They would think that she never had been happy before. Nay, then, she sets more store by the few nick-nacks Julius has given her than all I have bought her for twenty years. When yonder last bracelet came, she went on as if she had never seen aught of the kind in all her born days. Yet I have bought her one or two that cost more money, and happen more love, than it did. Eh? What, Charlotte?"

There were two large tears standing in his blue eyes, and two sprang into Charlotte's to meet them. She clasped his hand tight, and after a minute's silence said,—

"I have a lover, father; the best a girl ever had. Has he made any difference between you and me? Only that I love you better. You are my first love; the very first creature I remember, father. One summer day you had me in your arms in the garden. I recollect looking at you and knowing you. I think it was at that moment my soul found me."

"It was on a summer day, Charlotte? Eh? What?"

"And the garden was all roses, father; red with roses,—roses full of scent. I can smell them yet. The sunshine, the roses, the sweet air, your face,—I shall never, never forget that moment, father."

"Nor I. I was a very happy man in those days, Charlotte.

Young and happy, and full of hope. I thought my children were some new make of children. I could not have believed then, that they would ever give me a heartache, or have one themselves. And I had not a care. Money was very easy with me then: now it is middling hard to bring buckle and tongue together."

"When Sophia is married, we can begin and save a little. Mother and you and I can be happy without extravagances."

"To be sure, we can; but the trouble is, my saving will be the losing of all I have to send away. It is very hard, Charlotte, to do right at both ends. Eh? What?"

After this conversation, spring came on rapidly, and it was not long ere Charlotte managed to reach Up-Hill. She had not seen Ducie for several weeks, and she was longing to hear something of Stephen. "But if ill had come, ill would have cried out, and I would have heard tell;" she thought, as she picked her way among the stones and *debris* of the winter storms. The country was yet bare; the trees had no leaves, no nests, no secrets; but she could see the sap running into the branches, making them dark red, scarlet, or yellow as rods of gold. Higher up, the pines, always green, took her into their shade; into their calm spirit of unchangeableness, their equal light, their keen aromatic air. Then came the bare fell, and the raw north wind, and the low gray house, stretching itself under the leafless, outspreading limbs of the sycamores.

In the valley, there had been many wild flowers,—tufts of violets and early primroses,—and even at Up-Hill the blackthorn's stiff boughs were covered with tiny white buds, and here and there an open blossom. Ducie was in the garden at work; and as Charlotte crossed the steps in its stone wall she lifted her head, and saw her. Their meeting was free from all demonstration; only a smile, and a word or two of welcome, and yet how conscious of affection! How satisfied both women were! Ducie went on with her task, and Charlotte stood by her side, and watched her drop the brown seeds into the damp, rich earth; watched her clip the box-borders, and loosen the soil about the springing crocus bulbs. Here and there tufts of snowdrops were in full bloom,—white, frail bells, looking as if they had known only cheerless hours and cold sunbeams, and wept and shrank and feared through them.

As they went into the house, Ducie gathered a few; but at the threshhold, Charlotte turned, and saw them in her hand. A little fear and annoyance came into her face. "You a North-country woman, Ducie," she said, "and yet going to bring snowdrops across the doorstone? I would not have believed such a thing of you. Leave them outside the porch. Be said, now."

"It seems such a thing to think of flowers that way,—making them signs of sorrow."

"You know what you said about your father and the plant,—'Death-come-quickly.' I have heard snowdrops called 'flowers from dead-men's dale.' Look at them. They are like a shrouded corpse. They keep their heads always turned down to the grave. It is ill-luck to bring them where there is life and love and warmth. It will do you no harm to mind me; so be said, Ducie. Besides, I wouldn't pull them anyway. There was little Grace Lewthwaite, she was always gathering the poor, innocent flowers just to fling them on the dusty road to be trodden and trampled to pieces; well, before she was twelve years old, she faded away too. Perhaps even the prayers of mangled flowers may be heard by the merciful Creator."

"You do give me such turns, Charlotte." But who ever reasons with a superstition? Ducie simply obeyed Charlotte's wish, and laid the pallid blooms almost remorsefully back upon the earth from which she had taken them. A strange melancholy filled her heart; although the servants were busy all around, and everywhere she heard the good-natured laugh, the thoughtless whistle, or the songs of hearts at ease.

When she entered the houseplace she put the bright kettle on the hob, and took out her silver teapot and her best cups of lovely crown Derby. And as she moved about in her quiet, hospitable way they began to talk of Stephen. "Was he well?"—"Yes, he was well, but there were things that might be better. I thought when he went to Bradford," continued Ducie, "that he would at least be learning something that he might be the better of in the long end; and that in a mill he would over-get his notions about sheepskins being spun into golden fleeces. But he doesn't seem to get any new light that way, and Up-Hill is not doing well without him. Fold and farm are needing the master's eye and hand; and it will be a poor lambing season for us, I think, wanting Steve. And, deary me, Charlotte, one word from you would bring him home!"

Charlotte stooped, and lifted the tortoise-shell cat, lying on the rug at her feet. She was not fond of cats, and she was only attentive to puss as the best means of hiding her blushes. Ducie understood the small, womanly ruse, and waited no other answer. "What is the matter with the squire, Charlotte? Does he think that Stephen isn't good enough to marry you? I'll not say that Latrigg evens Sandal in all things, but I will say that there are very few families that can even Latrigg. We have been without reproach,—good women, honest men; not afraid of any face of clay, though it wore a crown above it."

"Dear Ducie, there is no question at all of that. The trouble arose about Julius Sandal. Father was determined that I or Sophia should marry him, and he was afraid of Steve standing in the way of Julius. As for myself, I felt as if Julius had been invited to Seat-Sandal that he might make his choice of us; and I took good care that he should understand from the first hour that I was not on his approbation. I resented the position on my own account, and I did not intend Stephen to feel that he was only getting a girl who had been appraised by Julius Sandal, and declined."

"You are a good girl, Charlotte; and as for Steve standing in the way of Julius Sandal, he will, perhaps, do that yet, and to some more purpose than sweet-hearting. I hear tell that he is very rich; but Steve is not poor,—no, not by a good deal. His grandfather and I have been saving for him more than twenty years, and Steve is one to turn his penny well and often. If you marry Steve, you will not have to study about money matters."

"Poor or rich, I shall marry Steve if he is true to me."

"There is another thing, Charlotte, a thing I talk about to no one; but we will speak of it once and forever. Have you heard a word about Steve's father? My trouble is long dead and buried, but there are some that will open the grave itself for a mouthful of scandal. What have you heard? Don't be afraid to speak out."

"I heard that you ran away with Steve's father."

"Yes, I did."

"That your father and mother opposed your marriage very much."

"Yes, that also is true."

"That he was a handsome lad, called Matt Pattison, your father's head shepherd."

"Was that all?"

"That it killed your mother."

"No, that is untrue. Mother died from an inflammation brought on by taking cold. I was no-ways to blame for her death. I was to blame for running away from my home and duty, and I took in full all the sorrowful wage I earned. Steve's father did not live to see his son; and when I heard of mother's death, I determined to go back to father, and stay with him always if he would let me. I got to Sandal village in the evening, and stayed with Nancy Bell all night. In the morning I went up the fell; it was a wet, cold morning, with gusts of wind driving the showers like a solid sheet eastward. We had a hard fight up the breast of the mountain; and the house looked bleak and desolate, for the men were all in the barn threshing, and the women in the kitchen at the butter-troughs. I stood in the porch to catch my breath, and take my plaid from around the child; and I heard father in a loud, solemn voice saying the Collect,—father always spoke in that way when he was saying the Confession or the Collect,—and I knew very well that he would be standing at that east window, with his prayer-book open on the sill. So I waited until I heard the 'Amen,' and then I lifted the latch and went in. He turned around and faced me; and his eyes fell at once upon little Steve, who was a bonny lad then, more than three years old. 'I have come back to you, father,' I said, 'I and my little Steve.'—'Where is thy husband?' he asked. I said, 'He is in the grave. I did wrong, and I am sorry, father.'"

"'Then I forgive thee.' That was all he said. His eyes were

Amelia E. Barr

fixed upon Steve, for he never had a son of his own; and he held out his hands, and Steve went straight to him; and he lifted the boy, and kissed him again and again, and from that moment he loved him with all his soul. He never cast up to me the wrong I had done; and by and by I told him all that had happened to me, and we never more had a secret between us, but worked together for one end; and what that end was, some day you may find out. I wish you would write a word or two to Steve. A word would bring him home, dear."

"But I cannot write it, Ducie. I promised father there should be no love-making between us, and I would not break a word that father trusts in. Besides, Stephen is too proud and too honorable to have any underhand courting. When he can walk in and out Seat-Sandal in dayshine and in dark, and as every one's equal, he will come to see me. Until then we can trust each other and wait."

"What does the squire think of Steve's plans? Maybe, now, they are not very pleasant to him. I remember at the sheep-shearing he did not say very much."

"He did not say very much because he never thought that Steve was in earnest. Father does not like changes, and you know how land-owners regard traders. And I'm sure you wouldn't even one of our shepherd-lads with a man that minds a loom. The brave fellows, travelling the mountain-tops in the fiercest storms to fold the sheep, or seek some stray or weakly lamb, are very different from the lank, white-faced mannikins all finger-ends for a bit of machinery; aren't they, Ducie? And I would far rather see Steve counting his flocks on the fells than his spinning-jennys in a mill. Father was troubled about the railway coming to Ambleside, and I do think a factory in Sandal-Side would make him heart-sick."

"Then Steve shall never build one while Sandal lives. Do you think I would have the squire made heart-sick if I could make him heart-whole? Not for all the woollen yarn in England. Tell him Ducie said so. The squire and I are old, old friends. Why, we pulled primroses together in the very meadow Steve thought of building in! I'm not the woman to put a mill before a friend, oh, no! And in the long end I think you are right, Charlotte. A man had better work among sheep than among human beings. They are a deal more peaceable and easy to get on with. It is not so very hard for a shepherd to be a good man."

"You speak as I like to hear you, Ducie; but I must be going, for a deal falls to my oversight now." And she rose quickly from the tea-table, and as she tied on her bonnet, began to sing,—

"'God bless the sheep upon the fells!
Oh, do you hear the tinkling bells
Of sheep that wander on the fells?

The tinkling bells the silence fills,
Sings cheerily the soul that wills;
God bless the shepherd on the hills!

God bless the sheep! Their tinkling bells
Make music over all the fells;
By *force* and *gill* and *tarn* it swells,
And this is what their music tells:
God bless the sheep upon the fells.'"

The melody was wild and simple, a little plaintive also; and Charlotte sang it with a low, sweet monotony that recalled, one knew not how or why, the cool fragrance of the hillside, and the scent of wild flowers by running water.

Amelia E. Barr

Then she went slowly home, Ducie walking to the pine-wood with her. There was a vague unrest and fear at her heart, she knew not why; for who can tell whence spring their thoughts, or what mover first starts them from their secret lodging-place? A sadness she could not fight down took possession of her; and it annoyed her the more, because she found every one pleasantly excited over a box of presents that had just arrived from India for Sophia. She knew that her depression would be interpreted by some as envy and jealousy, and she resented the false position it put her in; and yet she found it impossible to affect the enthusiasm which was expected from her over the Cashmere shawl and scarfs, the Indian fans and jewelry, the carved ivory trinkets, the boxes full of Eastern scents,—sandalwood and calamus, nard and attar of roses, and pungent gums that made the old "Seat" feel like a little bit of Asia.

In a few days Julius followed; he came to see the presents, and to read, with personal illustrations and comments, the letters that had accompanied them. Sophia's ideas of her own importance grew constantly more pronounced; indeed, there was a certain amount of "claim" in them, which no one liked very well to submit to. And yet it was difficult to resist demands enforced by such remarks as, "It is the last time I shall ask for such a thing;" "One expects their own people to take a little interest in their marriage;" "I am sure Julius and *his* family have done all *they* can;" "They seem to understand what a girl must feel and like at such an eventful time of her life," and so on, and so on, in variations suited to the circumstances or the occasion.

Every one was worn out before July, and every one felt it to be a relief when the wedding-day came. It was ushered in with the chiming of bells, and the singing of bride-songs by the village children. The village itself was turned upside down, and the house inside out. As for the gloomy old church, it looked like a festal place, with flowers and gay clothing and smiling faces. It was the express wish of Sophia that none of the company should wear white. "That distinction," she said, "ought to be reserved for the bride;" and among the maids in pink and blue and primrose, she stood a very lily of womanhood. Her diaphanous, floating robe of Dacca muslin; her Indian veil of silver tissue, filmy as light; her gleaming pearls and feathery fan, made her

"A sight to dream of, not to tell."

The service was followed by the conventional wedding-breakfast; the congratulations of friends, and the rattling away of the bridal-carriage to the "hurrahing" of the servants and the villagers; and the *tin-tin-tabula* of the wedding-peals. Before four o'clock the last guest had departed, and the squire stood with his wife and Charlotte weary and disconsolate amid the remains of the feast and the dying flowers; all of them distinctly sensitive to that mournful air which accomplished pleasures leave behind them.

The squire could say nothing to dispel it. He took his rod as an excuse for solitude, and went off to the fells. Mrs. Sandal was crying with exhaustion, and was easily persuaded to go to her room, and sleep. Then Charlotte called the servants, men and women, and removed every trace of the ceremony, and all that was unusual or extravagant. She set the simplest of meals; she managed in some way, without a word, to give the worried squire the assurance that all the folly and waste and hurryment were over for ever; and that his life was to fall back into a calm, regular, economical groove.

He drank his tea and smoked his pipe to this sense, and was happier than he had been for many a week.

"It is a middling good thing, Alice," he said, "that we have only one more daughter to marry. I should think a matter of three or four would ruin or kill a man, let alone a mother. Eh? What?"

"That is the blessed truth, William. And yet it is the pride of my heart to say that there never was such a bride or such a bridal in Sandal-Side before. Still, I am tired, and I feel just as if I had had a trouble. Come day, go day; at the long end, life is no better than the preacher called it—*vanity*."

"To be sure it is not. We laugh at a wedding, we cry at a burying, a christening brings us a feast. On the Sabbath we say our litany; and as for the rest of the year, one day marrows another."

"Well, well, William Sandal! Maybe we will both feel better after a night's sleep. To-morrow is untouched."

And the squire, looking into her pale, placid face, had not the heart to speak out his thought, which was, "Nay, nay; we have mortgaged to-morrow. Debt and fear, and the penalties of over-work and over-eating and over-feeling, will be dogging us for their dues by dayshine."

CHAPTER VIII

THE ENEMY IN THE HOUSEHOLD

"There is a method in man's wickedness,
It grows up by degrees."

"How sharper than a serpent's tooth it is
To have a thankless child!"

After the wedding, there were some weeks of that peaceful
monotony which is the happiest vehicle for daily life,—
weeks so uniform that Charlotte remembered their events as
little as she did their particular weather. The only circumstance that cast any shadow over them related to Harry. His
behavior had been somewhat remarkable, and the hope that
time would explain it had not been realized at the end of
August.

About three weeks before Sophia's marriage, Harry suddenly
wrote to say that he had obtained a three months' furlough, in
order to go to Italy with a sick friend. This letter, so utterly
unexpected, caused some heart-burning and disappointment.
Sophia had calculated upon Harry's fine appearance and
splendid uniform as a distinct addition to her wedding
spectacle. She also felt that the whole neighborhood would

be speculating upon the cause of his absence, and very likely infer from it that he disapproved of Julius; and the bare suspicion of such a slight made her indignant.

Julius considered this to be the true state of the case, though he promised himself "to find out all about Mr. Harry's affairs" as soon as he had the leisure and opportunity.

"The idea of Harry going as sick-nurse with any friend or comrade is absurd, Sophia. However, we can easily take Florence into our wedding-trip, only we must not let Charlotte know of our intention. Charlotte is against us, Sophia; and you may depend upon it, Harry meant to insult us by his absence."

Insult or not to the bride and bridegroom, it was a great disappointment to Mrs. Sandal. To see, to speak to Harry was always a sure delight to her. The squire loved and yet feared his visits. Harry always needed money; and lately his father had begun to understand, and for the first time in his life, what a many-sided need it was. To go to his secretary, and to find no gold pieces in its cash-drawer; and to his bank-book, and find no surplus credit there, gave the squire a feeling of blank amazement and heart-sick perplexity. He felt that such a change as that might prefigure other changes still more painful and frightsome.

Charlotte inclined to the same opinion as Julius, regarding her brother's sudden flight to Florence. She concluded that he had felt it impossible to congratulate his sister, or to simulate any fraternal regard for Julius; and her knowledge of facts made her read for "sick friend" "fair friend." It was, indeed, very likely that the beautiful girl, whose likeness Harry carried so near his heart, had gone to Florence; and that he had moved heaven and earth to follow her there. And when his own love-affairs were pressing and important, how was it likely that he could care for those of Julius and Sophia?

So, at intervals, they wondered a little about Harry's peculiar movement, and tried hard to find something definite below the surface words of his short letters. Otherwise, a great peace had settled over Seat-Sandal. Its hall-doors stood open all day long, and the August sunshine and the garden scents drifted in with the lights and shadows. Life had settled down into such simple ways, that it seemed to be always at rest. The hours went and came, and brought with them their little measure of duty and pleasure, both so usual and easy, that they took nothing from the feelings or the strength, and gave an infinite sense of peace and contentment.

One August evening they were in the garden; there had been several hot, clear days, and the harvesters were making the most of every hour. The squire had been in the field until near sunset, and now he was watching anxiously for the last wain. "We have the earliest shearing in Sandal-Side," he said. "The sickle has not been in the upper meadows yet, and if they finish to-night it will be a good thing. It's a fine moon for work. *A fine moon, God bless her!* Hark! There is the song I have been waiting for, and all's well, Charlotte." And they stood still to listen to the rumble of the wagon, and the rude, hearty chant that at intervals accompanied it:—

"Blest be the day that Christ was born!
The last sheaf of Sandal corn
Is well bound, and better shorn.
Hip, hip, hurrah!"

"Good-evening, squire." The speaker had come quickly around one of the garden hedges, and his voice seemed to fall out of mid-air. Charlotte turned, with eyes full of light, and a flush of color that made her exceedingly handsome.

"Well-a-mercy! Good-evening, Stephen. When did you get home? Nobody had heard tell. Eh? What?"

"I came this afternoon, squire; and as there is a favor you can do us, I thought I would ask it at once."

"Surely, Stephen. What can I do? Eh? What?"

"I hear your harvest is home. Can you spare us a couple of men? The wheat in Low Barra fields is ready for the sickle."

"Three men, four, if you want them. You cannot have too many sickles. Cut wheat while the sun shines. Eh? What? How is the lady at Up-Hill?"

"Mother is middling well, I'm obliged to you. I think she has failed though, since grandfather died."

"It is likely. She has been too much by herself. You should stay at home, Stephen Latrigg. A man's duty is more often there than anywhere else. Eh?"

"I think you are right now, squire." And then he blundered into the very statement that he ought to have let alone. "And I am not going to build the mill, squire,—not yet, at least. I would not do any thing to annoy you for the world."

The information was pleasant to Sandal; but he had already heard it, in its least offensive way, through Ducie and Charlotte. Steve's broad relinquishment demanded some acknowledgment, and appeared to put him under an obligation which he did not feel he had any right to acknowledge. He considered the building of a mill so near his own property a great social wrong, and why should he thank Stephen Latrigg for not committing it?

So he answered coldly, "You must take your own way, Stephen. I am an old man. I have had my say in my generation, maybe I haven't any right to meddle with yours. New men, new times." Then being conscious that he was a little ungenerous he walked off to Mrs. Sandal, and left the lovers together. Steve would have forgiven the squire a great deal more for such an opportunity, especially as a still kinder after-thought followed it. For he had not gone far before he turned, and called back, "Bring Steve into the house, Charlotte. He will stay, and have a bit of supper with us, no doubt." Perhaps the lovers made the way into the house a little roundabout. But Sandal was not an unjust man; and having given them the opportunity, he did not blame them for taking it. Besides he could trust Charlotte. Though the heavens fell, he could trust Charlotte.

During supper the conversation turned again to Stephen's future plans. Whether the squire liked to admit the fact or not, he was deeply interested in them; and he listened carefully to what the young man said.

"If I am going to trust to sheep, squire, then I may as well have plenty to trust to. I think of buying the Penghyll 'walk,' and putting a thousand on it."

"My song, Stephen!"

"I can manage them quite well. I shall get more shepherds, and there are new ways of doing things that lighten labor very much. I have been finding out all about them. I think of taking three thousand fleeces, at the very least, to Bradford next summer."

"Two hundred years ago somebody thought of harnessing a flock of wild geese for a trip to the moon. They never could do it. Eh? What?"

Stephen laughed a little uncomfortably. "That was nonsense, squire."

"It was 'almighty youth,' Stephen. The young think they can do every thing. In a few years they do what they can and what they may. It is a blessed truth that the mind cannot stay long in a *bree*. It gets tired of ballooning, and comes down to hands and feet again. Eh? What?"

"I think you mean kindly, squire."

The confidence touched him. "I do, Steve. Don't be in a hurry, my lad. There are some things in life that are worth a deal more than money,—things that money cannot buy. Let money take a backward place." Then he voluntarily asked about the processes of spinning and weaving wool, and in spite of his prejudices was a little excited over Stephen's startling statements and statistics.

Indeed, the young man was so interesting, that Sandal went with him to the hall-door, and stood there with him, listening to his graphic descriptions of the wool-rooms at the top of the great Yorkshire mills. "I'd like well to take you through one, squire. Fleeces? You would be wonder-struck. There are long staple and short staple; silky wool and woolly wool; black fleeces from the Punjaub, and curly white ones from Bombay; long warps from Russia, short ones from Buenos Ayres; little Spanish fleeces, and our own Westmoreland and Cumberland skins, that beat every thing in the world for size. And then to see them turned into cloth as fast as steam can do it! My word, squire, there never was magic or witchcraft like the steam and metal witchcraft of a Yorkshire mill."

"Well, well, Steve. I don't fret myself because I am set in stiller ways, and I don't blame those who like the hurryment of steam and metal. Each of us has God's will to do, and our own race to run; and may we prosper."

After this, Steve, sometimes gaining and sometimes losing, gradually won his way back to the squire's liking. September proved to be an unusually fair month; and to the lovers it was full of happiness, for early in it their relation to each other was fully recognized; and Stephen had gone in and out of the pleasant "Seat," dayshine and dark, as the acknowledged lover of Charlotte Sandal. The squire, upon the whole, submitted gracefully: he only stipulated that for some time, indefinitely postponed, the subject of marriage was not to be taken into consideration. "I could not bear it any road. I could not bear it yet, Stephen. Wait your full time, and be glad to wait. So few young men will understand that to pluck the blossom is to destroy the fruit."

Towards the end of September, there was a letter from Sophia dated Florence. Some letters are like some individuals, they carry with them a certain unpleasant atmosphere. None of Sophia's epistles had been very satisfactory; for they were so short, and yet so definitely pinned to Julius, that they were but commentaries on that individual. At Paris she had simply asked Julius, "What do *you* think of Paris?" And the opinion of Julius was then given to Seat-Sandal confidently as the only correct estimate that the world was likely to get. At Venice, Rome, Naples, her plan was identical; and any variation of detail simply referred to the living at different places, and how Julius liked it, and how it had agreed with him.

So when the Florence letter came, there was no particular enthusiasm about it. The address assigned it to the squire, and he left it lying on the table while he finished the broiled trout and coffee before him. But it troubled Charlotte, and she waited anxiously for the unpleasant words she felt sure were inside of it. Yet there was no change on the squire's face, and no sign of annoyance, as he read it. "It is about the usual thing, Alice. Julius likes Florence. It is called 'the beautiful.' Julius thinks that it deserves the title. The wine in Rome did not suit Julius, but he finds the Florence vintage much better. The climate is very delightful, Julius is sure he will derive benefit from it; and so on, and so on, and so on." Then there was a short pause, and a rapid turn of the sheet to glance at the other side. "Oh, Julius met Harry yesterday! He—Julius—does not think Harry is doing right. 'Harry always was selfish and extravagant, and though he did affront us on our wedding-day, Julius thought it proper to call upon him. He—I mean Harry—was with a most beautiful young girl. Julius thinks father ought to write to him, and tell him to go back to his duty.'"

These were the words, doubtful and suggestive, which made every heart in Seat-Sandal thoroughly uncomfortable. And yet Charlotte stoutly said, "I would not mind Sophia's insinuations, father and mother. She is angry at Harry. Harry has as much right in Florence as Sophia has. He told us he was going there. He has written to us frequently. Suppose he was with a beautiful girl: is Julius the only young man entitled to such a privilege? Sophia is happy in her own way, and we do not envy nor interfere with her happiness; but why should we permit her to make us unhappy? Throw the letter out of your memories, dear father and mother. It is only a piece of ill-nature. Perhaps Julius had been cross with her; and if Sophia has a grievance, she never rests until she passes it on to some one."

Women still hold the divining-cup, and Charlotte was not far wrong in her supposition. In spite of their twinship of soul, and in spite of that habit of loving which was involved in their belief "that they had been husband and wife in many a previous existence," Mr. and Mrs. Julius Sandal disagreed as conventionally as the ordinary husband and wife of one existence. The day on which the Florence letter was written had been a very unhappy one for Sophia. Julius had quarrelled with her about some very trivial affair, and had gone out in a temper disgracefully at variance with the occasion for it; and Sophia had sat all day nursing her wrath in her darkened room. She did not dress for the evening drive, for she had determined to "keep up" her anger until Julius made her some atonement.

But when he came home, she could not resist his air of confidence and satisfaction. He had quite forgotten the affair at the breakfast-table, and was only eager for her help and sympathy. "I have seen Harry," he said.

"Very well. You came here to find him. I suppose I can see him also. I am sure I need to see some one. I have been neglected all day; suffering, lonely,"—

"Sophia, you and I are here to look after our own affairs a little. If you are willing to help me, I shall be glad; if not"—

"You know I will help you in any thing I can, Julius."

Then he kissed her, and she cried a little, and he kissed her again; and she dressed herself, and they went for a drive, and during it met Harry, and brought him back to dine with them. Julius was particularly pleasant to the unsuspicious soldier. He soon perceived that he was thoroughly disgusted with the rigor and routine of military life, and longing to free himself from its thraldom; and he encouraged him in the idea.

"I wonder how you stand it, Harry," he said sympathetically.

"You see, Julius, when I went into the army, I was so weary of Sandal-Side; and I liked the uniform, and the stir of an officer's life, and the admiration of the girls, and the whole *eclat* of the thing. But when a man's time comes, and he falls so deeply in love that he cares for nothing on earth but one woman, then he hates whatever comes between himself and that woman."

"Naturally so. I suppose it is the young lady I saw you walking with this morning."

And Harry blushed like a girl as he gravely nodded his head.

"Does she live here?"

"She will for the future."

"And you must go back to your regiment?"

"Almost immediately."

"Too bad! Too bad! Why not leave the army?"

"I—I have thought of that; but unless I returned to Sandal-Side, my father would be angry beyond every thing."

"Fathers cannot be autocrats—quite. You might sell out."

"Julius, you ought not to suggest such a thing. The temptation has been lurking in my own heart. I am sorry you have given it a voice. It would be a shameful thing to do unless father were willing."

"I have a friend anxious for a commission. I should think a thousand pounds would make an exchange."

"Do not speak on the subject, Julius."

"Very well. I was only supposing; a fellow-feeling, you know. I have married the girl I desired; and I am sorry for a young man who is obliged to leave a handsome mistress, and to feel that others may see her and talk to her while he cannot. It was only a supposition. Do not mind it."

But the germ of every wrong deed is the reflection whether it be possible. And after Harry had gone away with the thought in his heart, Julius sat musing over his own plans, and Sophia wrote the letter which so unnecessarily and unkindly shadowed the pleasant life at Seat-Sandal. For though the squire pooh-poohed it, and Charlotte professed indifference about it, and Mrs. Sandal kept assuring herself and others that "Harry never, never would do any thing wrong or unkind, especially about a woman," every one was apprehensive and watchful. But at last, even suspicion tires of watching for events that never happen; and Sophia sent other letters, and made no mention of Harry; and the fear that had crouched at each home-heart slunk away into forgetfulness.

Into total forgetfulness. When Harry voluntarily came home for Christmas, no one coupled his visit with the remarks made by Sophia four months previously. They had not expected to see him, and the news of his advent barely reached the house before he followed it; for there was a heavy snow-storm, and the mail was sent forward with difficulty. So Mrs. Sandal was reading the letter announcing his visit when she heard his voice in the hall, and the joyful cry of Charlotte as she ran to meet him. And that night every one was too happy, too full of inquiry and information, to notice that Harry was under an unusual restraint. It did not even strike Charlotte until she awoke the next morning with all her faculties fresh and clear; then she felt, rather than understood, that there was something not quite right about Harry.

It was still snowing, and every thing was white; but the atmosphere of a quiet, happy Christmas was in the house.

There were smiling faces and good wishes at the breakfast-table, and the shifting lustres of blazing fires upon the dark walls and evergreens and wax-white mistletoe. And the wind brought a Christmas greeting from the bells of Furness and Torver, and Sandal-Side peal sent it on to Earlstower and Coniston. After breakfast they all went to church; and Harry saw, as in a dream, the sacred table spread with spotless cloth and silver cups and flagons, and the dim place decked with holly, and the smiling glance of welcome from his old acquaintances in the village. And he fell into a reverie which was not a Christmas reverie, and had it suddenly broken by his sister singing high and clear the carol the angels sung on the hills of Bethlehem,—"Glory be to God on high!" And the tears sprang into his eyes, and he looked stealthily at his father and mother, who were reverently listening; and said softly to himself, "I wish that I had never been born."

For he had come to tell his father news which he knew would shake the foundations of love and life; and he felt like a coward and a thief in delaying the explanation. "What right have I to this one day's more love?" he asked himself; and yet he could not endure to mar the holy, unselfish festival with the revelation of his own selfishness. As the day wore on, a sense of weariness and even gloom came with it. Rich food and wine are by no means conducive to cheerfulness. The squire sloomed and slept in his chair; and finally, after a cup of tea, went to bed. The servants had a party in their own hall, and Mrs. Sandal and Charlotte were occupied an hour or two in its ordering. Then the mother was thoroughly weary; and before it was quite nine o'clock, Harry and Charlotte were left alone by the parlor fire. Charlotte was a little dull also; for Steve had found it impossible to get down the mountain during the storm, and she missed him, and was constantly inclined to fall into short silences.

After one of them, she raised her eyes to Harry's face, and

was shocked by its expression. "Harry," she said, leaning forward to take his hand, "I am sure you are in trouble. What is it?"

"If I durst tell you, Charlotte!"

"Whatever you have dared to do, you may dare to tell me, Harry, I think."

"I have got married."

"Well, where is the harm? Is it to the lady whose picture you showed me?"

"Yes. I told you she was poor."

"It is a great pity she is poor. I am afraid we are getting poor too. Father was saying last week that he had been talking with Squire Beverley. Emily is to have fifteen thousand pounds. Father is feverishly anxious about you and Emily. Her fortune would be a great thing at Sandal, and father likes her."

"What is the use of talking about Emily? I have been married to Beatrice Lanza since last September."

"Such a strange name! Is it a Scotch name?"

"She is an Italian."

"Harry Sandal! What a shame!"

"Don't you think God made Italians as well as Englishmen?"

"That is not the question. God made Indians and negroes and all sorts of people. But he set the world in races, as he set races in families. He told the Jews to keep to themselves. He was angry when they intermarried with others. It always brought harm. What kind of a person is an Italian? They are papists, I know. The Pope of Rome is an Italian. O Harry, Harry, Harry! It will kill father and mother. But perhaps, as you met her in Edinburgh, she is a Protestant. The Scotch are all Protestants."

"Beatrice is a Roman Catholic, a very strict Roman Catholic. I had to marry her in a Romish church." He said the words rather defiantly, for Charlotte's attitude offended him; and he had reached that point when it was a reckless pleasure to put things at their worst.

"Then I am ashamed of you. The dear old rector! He married father and mother; he christened and confirmed you; you might be sure, that if you could not ask him to marry you, you had no business to marry at all."

"You said her face was like an angel's, and that you would love her, Charlotte."

"Oh, indeed! But I did not think the angel was an Italian angel and a Roman-Catholic angel. Circumstances alter cases. You, who have been brought up a good Church-of-England gentleman, to go over to the Pope of Rome!"

"I have not gone over to the Pope of Rome."

"All the same, Harry; all the same. And you know how father feels about that. Father would fight for the Church quicker than he would fight for his own house and land. Why! the Sandals got all of their Millom Estate for being good Protestants; for standing by the Hanoverian line instead of those popish Stuarts. Father will think you have committed an act of treason against both church and state, and he will be ashamed to show his face among the Dale squires. It is too bad! too bad for any thing!" and she covered her face, and cried bitterly.

"She is so lovely, so good"—

"Nonsense! Were there no lovely English girls? no good English girls? Emily is ten times lovelier."

"You know what you said."

"I said it to please you."

"Charlotte!"

"Yes, I did,—at least, in a great measure. It is easy enough to call a pretty girl an angel; and as for my promise to love your wife, of course I expected you would choose a wife suitable to your religion and your birth. Suppose you selected some outlandish dress,—an Italian brigand's, for instance,—what would the neighboring gentlemen think of you? It would be an insult to their national costume, and they would do right to resent it. Well, being who and what you are, you have no right to bring an Italian woman into Seat-Sandal. It is an insult to every woman in the county, and they will make you feel it."

"I shall not give them the opportunity. Beatrice cannot live in this beastly climate."

"The climate is wrong also? Naturally. It would follow the religion and the woman. Harry Sandal, I wish I had died, ere my ears had heard such a shame and sorrow for my father and mother! Where are you going to live, then?"

"In Florence. It is the birthplace of Beatrice the city

associated with all her triumphs."

"God have mercy, Harry! Her triumphs! Is she, then, an actress?"

"She is a singer,—a wonderful singer; one to whom the world has listened with breathless delight."

"A singing woman! And you have married her? It is an outrage on your ancestors, and on your parents and sisters."

"I will not hear you speak in that way, Charlotte. Of course I married her. Did you wish me to ruin and debase her? *That*, I suppose, you could have forgiven. My sin against the Sandals and society is, that I married her."

"No, sir; you know better. Your sin is in having any thing whatever to do with her. There is not a soul in Sandal that would have hesitated between ruin and marriage. If it had to be one or the other, then father and mother both, then I, then all your friends, would have said without hesitation, 'Marry the woman.'"

"I expected and hoped this would be your view of the situation. I could not give up Beatrice, and I could not be a scoundrel to her."

"You might have thought of another woman besides Beatrice. Is a sin against a mother a less sin than one against a strange woman? A mother is something sacred. To wound her heart is to throw a stone at her. You have committed a sort of sacrilege. And you are married. No entreaties can prevent, and no repentance can avail. Oh, what a sorrow to darken all the rest of father's and mother's days! What right have you to spoil their lives, in order to give yourself a little pleasure? O Harry! I never knew that you were selfish before."

"I deserve all you say, Charley, but I loved Beatrice so much."

"Are you sure, even of that excuse? I heard you vow that you loved Eliza Pierson 'so much,' and Fanny Ulloch 'so much,' and Emily Beverley 'so much.' Why did you not come home, and speak to me before it was too late? Why come at all now?"

"Because I want to talk to you about money. I have sold out."

"Sold out? Is there any more bad news? Do you know what father paid for your commission? Do you know how it hampered him to do it? that, in fact, he has never been quite easy about ready money since?"

"I had to sell out. Did I not tell you that Beatrice could not live in this climate? She was very ill when she returned to Italy. Signor Lanza was in great trouble about her."

"Signor Lanza? Her brother, I suppose."

"You suppose wrong. He is her father."

"For her, then, you have given up your faith, your country, your home, your profession, every thing that other men hold dear and sacred. Do you expect father to support you? Or is your wife to sing in Italy?"

"I think you are trying how disagreeable you can be, Charlotte."

"I am asking you honest questions in honest words."

"I have the money from the sale of my commission."

"It does not then strike you as dishonorable to keep it?"

"No, father gave me it."

"It appears to me, that if money was taken from the estate, let us say to stock a sheep-walk, and it was decided after three years' trial to give up the enterprise, and sell the sheep, that the money would naturally go back to the estate. When you came of age, father made you a very generous allowance. After a time you preferred that he should invest a large sum in a military commission for you; and you proposed to live upon your pay,—a thing you never have even tried to do. Suddenly, you find that the commission will not suit your more recent plans, and you sell it. Ought not the money to go back to the estate, and you to make a fresh arrangement with father about your allowance? That is my idea."

"Foolishness! And pray what allowance would my father make me, after the marriage I have contracted?"

"Now, you show your secret heart, Harry. You know you have no right to expect one, and so you keep what is not yours. This sin also for the woman whom you have put before every sentiment of love and honor."

"You were stubborn enough about Steve Latrigg."

"I was honorable; I was considerate for father, and did not put Stephen before him. Do you think I would ever marry Stephen against father's wish, or to the injury or suffering of any one whom I love? Certainly I would marry no one else, but I gave father my word that I would wait for his sanction. When people do right, things come right for them. But if father had stood out twenty years, Steve and I would have waited. Ducie gave us the same advice. 'Wait, children,' she said: 'I have seen many a wilful match, and many a run-away match, but never one, never one that prospered.'"

"Charley, I expected you to stand by me. I expected you to help me."

"O Harry, Harry! How can I help? What can I do? There is nothing left but to suffer."

"There is this: plead for me when I am away. My wife is sick in Florence. I must go to her at once. The money I have from my commission is all I have. I am going to invest it in a little house and vineyard. I have found out that my real tastes are for a pastoral life."

"Ah, if you could only have found that out for father!"

"Circumstances may change."

"That is, your father may die. I suppose you and your wife have talked over that probability. Beatrice will be able to endure the climate then."

"If I did not see that you were under very strong excitement, Charlotte, I should be much offended by what you say. But you don't mean to hurt me. Do you imagine that I feel no sorrow in leaving father and my mother and you and the old home? My heart is very sad to-night, Charley. I feel that I shall come here no more."

"Then why go away? Why, why?"

"Because a man leaves father and mother and every thing for the woman he loves. Charley, help me."

She shook her head sadly.

Amelia E. Barr

"Help me to break the trouble to father."

"There is no 'breaking' it. It will break him. It will kill him. Alas, it is the ungrateful child that has the power to inflict a slow and torturing death! Poor father! Poor mother! And it is I that must witness it. I, that would die to save them from such undeserved sorrow."

Then Harry rose up angrily, pushed his chair impatiently away, and without a word went to his own room.

In the morning the squire came down to breakfast in exceedingly high spirits. A Scotchman would have called him "*fey*," and been certain that misfortune was at his heels. And Charlotte looked at him in wondering pity, for Harry's face was the face of a man determined to carry out his own will regardless of consequences.

"Come, come, Harry," said the squire in a loud, cheerful voice, "you are moping, and eating no breakfast. Charlotte will have to fill three times before it is 'cup down' with me. I think we will take Dobbin, and go over to Windermere in the tax-cart. The roads will be a bit sloppery, but Dobbin isn't too old to splash through them at a rattling pace. He is a famous good old-has-been is Dobbin. Give me a Suffolk Punch for a roadster. I set much by them. Eh? What?"

"I must leave Sandal this morning, sir."

"Sir me no sir, Harry. 'Father' will stand between you and me, I think. You must make a put-off for one day. I was at Bowness last week, and they say such a winter for char-fishing was never seen. While I was on the lakeside, Kit Noble's boat came in. He had all of twenty dozen in the bottom of it. Mr. Wordsworth was there too, and he made a piece of poetry about 'The silvery lights playing over them;'

and he took me to see a picture that a London gentleman painted of Kit and his boat. You never saw fish out of the water look so fresh; their olive-green backs and vermillion bellies and dark-red fins were as natural as life. Come Harry, we will go and fetch over a few dozen. If you carry your colonel some, he will take the gift as an excuse for the day. Eh? What?"

"I think Harry had better not go with you, father."

"Eh? What is the matter with you, Charlotte? You are as nattert and cross as never was. Where is your mother? I like my morning cup filled with a smile. It helps the day through."

"Mother isn't feeling well. She had a bad dream about Harry and you, and she is making herself sick over it. She is all in a tremble. I didn't think mother was so foolish."

"Dreams are from somewhere beyond us, Charlotte. There's them that visit us a-dreaming. I am not so wise as to be foolish. I believe in some things that are outside of my short wits. Maybe we had better not go to Windermere. We might be tempted into a boat, and dry land is a middling bit safer. Eh? What?"

Charlotte felt as if she could endure her father's unsuspicious happiness no longer. It was like watching a little child smiling and prattling on the road to its mother's funeral. She put Mrs. Sandal's breakfast on a small tray, and with this in her hand went up-stairs, leaving Harry and the squire still at the table.

"Charlotte is a bit hurrysome this morning," he said; and Harry making no answer, he seemed suddenly to be struck with his attitude. He looked curiously at him a moment, and then lapsed into silence. "Harry wants money." That was his first thought, and he began to calculate how far he was able to meet the want. Even then, his only bitter reflection was, that Harry should suppose it necessary to be glum about it. "A cheerful asker is the next thing to a cheerful giver;" and to such musings he filled his pipe, and with a shadow of offence on his large ruddy face went into "the master's room" to smoke.

When kindly good-nature is snubbed, it feels it keenly; and there was a mist of tears in the squire's blue eyes when Harry followed, and he turned them on him. And it was part of his punishment, that, even in the first flush of the pleasure of his sin, he felt all the pangs of remorse.

"Father?"

"Well, well, Harry! I see you are wanting money again."

"It will be the last time. I am married, and am going to Italy to live."

"Eh? What?" The squire flushed hotly. His hand shook, his long clay pipe fell to the hearthstone, and was shattered to pieces.

Then a reckless desire to have the whole wrong out urged the unhappy son to a most cruel distinctness of detail. Without wasting a word in explanation or excuse, he stated broadly that he had fallen in love with the famous singer, Beatrice Lanza, and had married her. He spared himself or his father nothing; he appeared to gather a hard courage as he spoke of her failing health, her hatred of England, her devotion to her own faith, and the necessity of his retirement to Italy with her. He seemed determined to put it out of the power of any one to say worse of him than he had already said of himself.

In conclusion he added, "I have sold my commission, and paid what I owed, and have very little money left. Life, however, is not an expensive affair in the village to which I am going. If you will allow me two hundred pounds a year I shall be very grateful."

"I will not give you one penny, sir."

The words came thick and heavy, and with great difficulty; though the wretched father had risen, and was standing by the table, leaning hard with both hands upon it.

He would not look at his son, though the young man went on speaking. He heard nothing that he said. In his ears there was the roaring of mighty waters. All the waves and the billows were going over him. For a few moments he struggled desperately with the black, advancing tide. His sight failed, it was growing dark. Then he threw the last forces of life into one terrible cry, and fell, as a great tree falls, heavily to the ground.

The cry rang through the house. The mother, trembling in her bed; Charlotte, crouching upon the stairs, fearing and listening; the servants, chattering in the kitchen and the chambers,—all heard it, and were for a moment horrified by the agony and despair it expressed. But ere the awful echo had quite subsided, Charlotte was at her father's side; in a moment afterwards, Mrs. Sandal, sobbing at every flying step, and still in her night-clothing, followed; and then servants from every quarter came rushing to the master's room.

There was no time for inquiry or lamentation. Harry and two of the men mounted swift horses in search of medical help. Others lifted the insensible man, and carried him tenderly to his bed. In a moment the atmosphere of the house had changed. The master's room, which had held for generations nothing but memories of pastoral business and sylvan pleasures, had suddenly become a place of sorrow. The shattered pipe upon the hearthstone made Charlotte utter a low, hopeless cry of pain. She closed the shutters, and put the burning logs upon the hearth safely together, and then locked the door. Alas! alas! they had carried the master out, and in Charlotte's heart there was a conviction that he would never more cross its threshold.

After Harry's first feelings of anguish and horror had subsided, he was distinctly resentful. He felt his father's suffering to be a wrong to him. He began to reflect that the day for such intense emotions had passed away. But he forgot that the squire belonged to a generation whose life was filled and ruled by a few strong, decided feelings and opinions that struck their roots deep into the very foundations of existence; a generation, also, which was bearing the brunt of the transition between the strong, simple life of the past, and the rapid, complex life of the present. Thus the squire opposed to the indifference of the time a rigidity of habits, which, to even small events, gave that exceptional character which rarity once imparted. He felt every thing deeply, because every thing retained its importance to him. He had great reverence. He loved, and he hated. All his convictions and prejudices were for life.

Harry's marriage had been a blow at the roots of all his conscious existence. The Sandals had always married in their own county, Cumberland ladies of honorable pedigree, good daughters of the Church of England, good housewives, gentle and modest women, with more or less land and gold as their dowry. Emily Beverley would have been precisely such a wife. And in a moment, even while Harry was speaking, the squire had contrasted this Beatrice Lanza with her;—a foreigner,—an Italian, of all foreigners most objectionable; a subject of the Papal States; a member of the

Romish Church; a woman of obscure birth, poor and portionless, and in ill-health; worse than all, a public woman, who had sung for money, and yet who had made Harry desert his home and country and profession for her. And with this train of thought another ran parallel,—the shame and the wrong of it all. The disgrace to his wife and daughters, the humiliation to himself. Each bitter thought beat on his heart like the hammer on the anvil. They fought and blended with each other. He could not master one. He felt himself being beaten to the ground. He made agonizing efforts to retain control over the surging wave of anguish, rising, rising, rising from his breast to his brain. And failing to do so, he fell with the mighty cry of one who, even in the death agony, protests against the victor.

The news spread as if all the birds in the air carried it. There were a dozen physicians in Seat-Sandal before noon. There was a crowd of shepherds around it, waiting in silent groups for their verdict. All the afternoon the gentlemen of the Dales were coming and going with offers of help and sympathy; and in the lonely parlor the rector was softly pacing up and down, muttering, as he walked, passages from the "Order for the Visitation of the Sick":—

"O Saviour of the world, who by thy cross and precious blood hast redeemed us, save us, and help us, we humbly beseech thee, O Lord."

"Spare us good Lord. Spare thy people whom thou hast redeemed with thy most precious blood."

"Shut not up thy tender mercies in displeasure; but make him to hear of joy and gladness."

"Deliver him from the fear of the enemy. Lift up the light of thy countenance upon him. Amen."

CHAPTER IX

ESAU

"To be weak is miserable,
Doing or suffering."

"Now conscience wakes despair
That slumberd; wakes the bitter memory
Of what he was, what is, and what must be."

It was the middle of February before Harry could leave Sandal-Side. He had remained there, however, only out of that deference to public opinion which no one likes to offend; and it had been a most melancholy and anxious delay. He was not allowed to enter the squire's room, and indeed he shrank from the ordeal. His mother and Charlotte treated him with a reserve he felt to be almost dislike. He had been so accustomed to consider mother-love sufficient to cover all faults, that he forgot there was a stronger tie; forgot that to the tender wife the husband of her youth—her lover, friend, companion—is far nearer and dearer than the tie that binds her to sons and daughters.

Also, he did not care to give any consideration to the fact, that both his mother and Charlotte resented the kind of daughter and sister he had forced upon them. So there was little sympathy with him at Seat-Sandal, and he fancied that all the gentlemen of the neighborhood treated him with a perceptible coolness of manner. Perhaps they did. There are social intuitions, mysterious in their origin, and yet hitting singularly near the truth. Before circumstances permitted him to leave Sandal-Side, he had begun to hate the Seat and the neighborhood, and every thing pertaining to it, with all his heart.

The only place of refuge he had found had been Up-Hill. The day after the catastrophe he fought his way there, and with passionate tears and complaints told Ducie the terrible story. Ducie had some memories of her own wilful marriage, which made her tolerant with Harry. She had also been accused of causing her mother's death; and though she knew herself to be innocent, she had suffered by the accusation. She understood Harry's trouble as few others could have done; and though a good deal of his evident misery was on account of his separation from Beatrice, Ducie did not suspect this, and really believed the young man to be breaking his heart over the results of his rash communication.

He was agreeably surprised, also, to find that Stephen treated him with a consideration he had never done when he was a dashing officer, with all his own small world at his feet. For when any man was in trouble, Steve Latrigg was sure to take that man's part. He did not ask too particularly into the trouble. He had a way of saying to Ducie, "There will be faults on both sides. If two stones knock against each other until they strike fire, you may be sure both of them have been hard, mother. Any way, Harry is in trouble, and there is none but us to stand up for him."

But in spite of Steve's constant friendship, and Ducie's never-failing sympathy, Harry had a bad six weeks. There were days during them when he stood in the shadow of death, with almost the horror of a parricide in his heart. Long, lonely days, empty of every thing but anxiety and weariness. Long, stormy days, when he had not even the relief of a walk to Up-Hill. Days in which strangers slighted him. Days in which his mother and Charlotte could not even bear to see him. Days in which he fancied the servants disliked and neglected him. He was almost happy one afternoon when Stephen met him on the hillside, and said, "The squire is much better. The doctors think he is in no immediate danger. You might go to your wife, Harry, I should say."

"I am glad, indeed, to hear the squire is out of danger. And I long to go to my sick wife. I get little credit for staying here. I really believe, Steve, that people accuse me of waiting to step into father's shoes. And yet if I go away they will say things just as cruel and untrue."

But he went away before day-dawn next morning. Charlotte came down-stairs, and served his coffee; but Mrs. Sandal was watching the squire, who had fallen into a deep sleep. Charlotte wept much, and said little; and Harry felt at that hour as if he were being very badly treated. He could scarcely swallow; and the intense silence of the house made every slight noise, every low word, so distinct and remarkable, that he felt the constraint to be really painful.

"Well," he said, rising in haste, "I may as well go without a kind word. I am not to have one, apparently."

"Who is here to speak it? Can father? or mother? or I? But you have that woman."

"Good-by, Charley."

She bit her lips, and wrung her hands; and moaning like

some wounded creature lifted her face, and kissed him.

"Good-by. Fare you well, poor Harry."

A little purse was in his hand when she took her hand away; a netted silk one that he had watched the making of, and there was the glimmer of gold pieces through it. With a blush he put it in his pocket, for he was sorely pressed for money; and the small gift was a great one to him. And it almost broke his heart. He felt that it was all she could give him,—a little gold for all the sweet love that had once been his.

His horse was standing ready saddled. 'Osttler Bill opened the yard-gate, and lifted the lantern above his head, and watched him ride slowly away down the lane. When he had gone far enough to drown the clatter of the hoofs he put the creature to his mettle, and Bill waved the lantern as a farewell. Then, as it was still dark, he went back to the stable and lay down to sleep until the day broke, and the servants began to open up the house.

When Harry reached Ambleside it was quite light, and he went to the Salutation Inn, and ordered his breakfast. He had been a favorite with the landlady all his life long, and she attended to his comfort with many kindly inquiries and many good wishes. "And what do you think now, Capt. Sandal? Here has been a man from Up-Hill with a letter for you."

"Is he gone?"

"That he is. He would not wait, even for a bite of good victuals. He was dryish, though, and I gave him a glass of beer. Then him and his little Galloway took themselves off, without more words about it. Here it is, and Mr. Latrigg's writing on it or I wasn't christened Hannah Stavely."

Harry opened it a little anxiously; but his heart lightened as he read,—

DEAR HARRY,—If you show the enclosed slip of paper to your old friend Hannah Stavely, she will give you a hundred pounds for it. That is but a little bit of the kindness in mother's heart and mine for you. At Seat-Sandal I will speak up for you always, and I will send you a true word as to how all gets on there. God bless the squire, and bring you and him together again!

Your friend and brother,

STEPHEN LATRIGG.

And so Harry went on his way with a lighter heart. Indeed, he was not inclined at any time to share sorrow out of which he had escaped. Every mile which he put between himself and Sandal-Side gave back to him something of his old gay manner. He began first to excuse himself, then to blame others; and in a few hours he was in very comfortable relations with his own conscience; and this, not because he was deliberately cruel or wicked, but because he was weak, and loved pleasure, and considered that there was no use in being sorry when sorrow was neither a credit to himself, nor a compliment to others. And so to Italy and to love he sped as fast as money and steam could carry him. And on the journey he did his very best to put out of his memory the large, lonely, gray "Seat," with its solemn, mysterious chamber of suffering, and its wraiths and memories and fearful fighting away of death.

But on the whole, the hope which Stephen had given him of the squire's final recovery was a too flattering one. There was, perhaps, no immediate danger of death, but there was still less prospect of entire recovery. He had begun to remember a little, to speak a word or two, to use his hands in the weak, uncertain way of a young child; but in the main he lay like a giant, bound by invisible and invincible bonds; speechless, motionless, seeking through his large, pathetic eyes the help and comfort of those who bent over him. He had quite lost the fine, firm contour of his face, his ruddy color was all gone; indeed, the country expression of "face of clay," best of all words described the colorless, still countenance amid the white pillows in the darkened room.

As the spring came on he gained strength and intelligence, and one lovely day his men lifted him to a couch by the window. The lattices were flung wide open, that he might see the trees tossing about their young leaves, and the grass like grass in paradise, and hear the bees humming among the apple-blooms, and the sheep bleating on the fells. The earth was full of the beauty and the tranquillity of God. The squire looked long at the familiar sights; looked till his lips trembled, and the tears rolled heavily down his gray face. And then he realized all that he had suffered, he remembered the hand that had dealt him the blow. And while Mrs. Sandal was kissing away his tears, and speaking words of hope and love, a letter came from Sophia.

It was dated Calcutta. Julius had taken her there in the winter, and the news of her father's illness did not reach her for some weeks. But, as it happened, when Charlotte's letter detailing the sad event arrived, Julius was particularly in need of something to wonder over and to speculate about; and of all subjects, Seat-Sandal interested him most. To be master of the fine old place was his supreme ambition. He felt that he possessed all the qualities necessary to make him a leader among the Dales gentlemen. He foresaw, through them, social influence and political power; and he had an ambition to make his reign in the house of Sandal the era of a new and far more splendid dynasty.

He had been lying in the shade, drinking iced coffee, and smoking. But as Sophia read, he sat upright, and a look of speculation came into his eyes. "There is no use weeping, my love," he said languidly, "you will only dim your beauty, and that will do neither your father nor me any good. Let us go to Sandal. Charlotte and mother must be worn out, and we can be useful at such a time. I think, indeed, our proper place is there. The affairs of the 'walks' and the farms must be attended to, and what will they do on quarter-day? Of course Harry will not remain there. It would be unkind, wrong, and in exceedingly bad taste."

"Poor, dear father! And oh, Julius, what a disgrace to the family! A singer! How could Harry behave so shamefully to us all?"

"Harry never cared for any mortal but himself. How disgracefully he behaved about our marriage; for this same woman's sake, I have no doubt. You must remember that I disapproved of Harry from the very first. The idea of terminating a *liaison* of that kind with a marriage! Harry ought to be put out of decent society. You and I ought to be at Seat-Sandal now. Charlotte will be pushing that Stephen Latrigg into the Sandal affairs, and you know what I think of Stephen Latrigg. He is to be feared, too, for he has capabilities, and Charlotte to back him; and Charlotte was always underhand, Sophia. You would not see it, but she was. Order your trunks to be packed at once,—don't forget the rubies my mother promised you,—and I will have a conversation with the judge."

Judge Thomas Sandal was by no means a bad fellow. He had left Sandal-Side under a sense of great injustice, but he had done well to himself; and those who had done him wrong, had disappeared into the cloud of death. He had forgotten all his grievances, he had even forgotten the inflicters of them.

He had now a kindly feeling towards Sandal, and was a little proud of having sprung from such a grand old race. Therefore, when Julius told him what had happened, and frankly said he thought he could buy from Harry Sandal all his rights of succession to the estate, Judge Thomas Sandal saw nothing unjust in the affair.

The law of primogeniture had always appeared to him a most unjust and foolish law. In his own youth it had been a source of burning anger and dispute. He had always declared it was a shame to give Launcelot every thing, and William and himself scarce a crumb off the family loaf. To his eldest brother, as his eldest brother, he had declined to give "honor and obedience." "William is a far finer fellow," he said one day to his mother; "far more worthy to follow father than Launcie is. If there is any particular merit in keeping up the old seat and name, for goodness' sake let father choose the best of us to do it!" For such revolutionary and disrespectful sentiments he had been frequently in disgrace; and the end of the disputing had been his own expatriation, and the founding of a family of East-Indian Sandals.

He heard Julius with approval. "I think you have a very good plan," he said. "Harry Sandal, with his play-singing wife, would have a very bad time of it among the Dalesmen. He knows it. He will have no desire to test the feeling. I am sure he will be glad to have a sum of ready money in lieu of such an uncomfortable right. As for the Latriggs, my mother always detested them. Sophia and you are both Sandals; certainly, your claim would be before that of a Charlotte Latrigg."

"Harry, too, is one of those men who are always poor, always wanting money. I dare say I can buy his succession for a song."

"No, no. Give him a fair price. I never thought much of Jacob buying poor Esau out for a mess of pottage. It was a mean trick. I will put ten thousand pounds at Bunder's in Threadneedle Street, London, for you. Draw it all if you find it just and necessary. The rental ought to determine the value. I want you to have Seat-Sandal, but I do not want you to steal it. However, my brother William may not die for many a year yet; those Dale squires are a century-living race."

In accordance with these plans and intentions, Sophia wrote. Her letter was, therefore, one of great and general sympathy; in fact, a very clever letter indeed. It completely deceived every one. The squire was told that Sophia and Julius were coming, and his face brightened a little. Mrs. Sandal and Charlotte forgot all but their need of some help and comfort which was family help and comfort, free of ceremony, and springing from the same love, hopes, and interests.

Stephen, however, foresaw trouble. "Julius will get the squire under his finger," he said to Charlotte. "He will make himself indispensable about the estate. As for Sophia, she could always work mother to her own purposes. Mother obeyed her will, even while she resented and disapproved her authority. So, Charlotte, I shall begin at once to build Latrigg Hall. I know it will be needed. The plan is drawn, the site is chosen; and next Monday ground shall be broken for the foundation."

"There is no harm in building your house, Steve. If father should die, mother and I would be here upon Harry's sufferance. He might leave the place in our care, he might bring his wife to it any day."

"And how could you live with her?"

"It would be impossible. I should feel as if I were living with my father's—with the one who really gave father the death-blow."

So when Julius and Sophia arrived at Seat-Sandal, the walls of Latrigg Hall were rising above the green sod. A most beautiful site had been chosen for it,—the lowest spur on the western side of the fell; a charming plateau facing the sea, shaded with great oaks, and sloping down into a little dale of lovely beauty. The plan showed a fine central building, with lower wings on each side. The wide porches, deep windows, and small stone balconies gave a picturesque irregularity to the general effect. This home had been the dream of Stephen's manhood, and Ducie also had urged him to its speedy realization; for she knew that it was the first step towards securing for himself that recognition among the county gentry which his wealth and his old family entitled him to. Not that there was any intention of abandoning Up-Hill. Both would have thought such a movement a voluntary insult to the family wraiths,—one sure to bring upon them disaster of every kind. Up-Hill was to be Ducie's residence as long as she lived; it was to be always the home of the family in the hot months, and thus retain its right as an integral part and portion of the Latriggs' hearth.

"I have seen the plan of Latrigg Hall," said Julius one day to Sophia. "An absurdly fine building for a man of Stephen's birth. What will he do with it? It will require as large an income as Seat-Sandal to support it."

"Stephen is rich. His grandfather left him a great deal of money. Ducie will add considerably to the sum, and Stephen seems to have the faculty of getting it. My mother says he is managing three 'walks,' and all of them are doing well."

"Nevertheless, I do not like him. 'In-law' kinsmen and

kinswomen are generally detestable. Look at my brothers-in-law, Mr. Harry Sandal and Mr. Stephen Latrigg; and my sisters-in-law, Mrs. Harry Sandal and Miss Charlotte Sandal; a pretty undesirable quartette I think."

"And look at mine. For sisters-in-law, Mahal and Judith Sandal; for brothers-in-law, William and Tom Sandal; a pretty undesirable quartette I think."

Julius did not relish the retort; for he replied stiffly, "If so, they are at least at the other end of the world, and not likely to trouble you. That is surely something in their favor."

The first movement of the Julius Sandals in Seat-Sandal had been a clever one. "I want you to let us have the east rooms, dear mother," said Sophia, on their arrival; "Julius does feel the need of the morning sun so much." And though other rooms had been prepared, the request was readily granted, and without any suspicion of the motive which had dictated it. And yet they had made a very prudent calculation. Occupying the east rooms gave them a certain prominence and standing in the house, for only guests of importance were assigned to them; and the servants, who are people of wise perceptions generally, took their tone from the circumstance.

It seemed as if a spirit of dissatisfaction and quarrelling came with them. The maids all found out that their work was too heavy, and that they were worn out with it. Sophia had been pitying them. "Mrs. Sandal does not mean to be hard, but she is so wrapped up in the squire she sees nothing; and Miss Charlotte is so strong herself, she really expects too much from others. She does not intend to be exacting, but then she is; she can't help it."

And sitting over "a bit of hot supper" the chambermaid

repeated the remark; and the housemaid said she only knew that she was traipsed off her feet, and hadn't been near hand her own folks for a fortnight; and the cook thought Missis had got quite nattry. She had been near falling out with her more than once; and all the ill-nature was because she was fagged out, all day long and every day making some kind of little knick-shaw or other that was never eaten.

Not one remembered that the Julius Sandals had themselves considerably increased the work of the house; and that Mrs. Julius alone could find quite sufficient employment for one maid. Since her advent, Charlotte's room had been somewhat neglected for the fine guest-chambers; but it was upon Charlotte all the blame of over-work and weariness was laid. Insensibly the thought had its effect. She began to feel that for some reason or other she was out of favor; that her few wants were carelessly attended to, and that Mrs. Julius influenced the house as completely as she had done when she was Miss Sandal.

She soon discovered, also, that repining was useless. Her mother begged for peace at any cost. "Put up with it," she said, "for a little while, Charlotte. I cannot bear quarrelling. And you know how Sophia will insist upon explaining. She will call up the servants, and 'fend and prove,' and make complaints and regrets, and in the long end have all on her own side. And I can tell you that Ann has been queer lately, and Elizabeth talks of leaving at Martinmas. O Charlotte! put up with things, my dear. There is only you to help me."

Charlotte could not resist such appeals. She knew she was really the hand to which all other hands in the house looked, the heart on which her father and mother leaned their weary hearts; still, she could not but resent many an unkind position, which Sophia's clever tactics compelled her to take. For instance, as she was leaving the room one morning,

Sophia said in her blandest voice, "Dear Charlotte, will you tell Ann to make one of those queen puddings for Julius. He does enjoy them so much."

Ann did not receive the order pleasantly. "They are a sight of trouble, Miss Charlotte. I'll be hard set with the squire's fancies to-day. And there is as good as three dinners to make now, and I must say a queen's pudding is a bit thoughtless of you." And Charlotte felt the injustice she was too proud to explain to a servant. But even to Sophia, complaint availed nothing. "You must give extra orders yourself to Ann in the future," she said. "Ann accuses me of being thoughtless in consequence of them."

"As if I should think of interfering in your duties, Charlotte. I hope I know better than that. You would be the first to complain of my 'taking on' if I did, and I should not blame you. I am only a guest here now. But I am sure a little queen pudding is not too much to ask, in one's own father's house too. Julius has not many fancies I am sure, but such a little thing."

"Julius can have all the fancies he desires, only do please order them from Ann yourself."

"Well, I never! I am sure father and mother would never oppose a little pudding that Julius fancies."

Does any one imagine that such trials as these are small and insignificant? They are the very ones that make the heart burn, and the teeth close on the lips, and the eyes fill with angry tears. They take hope out of daily work, and sunshine out of daily life, and slay love as nothing else can slay it. There was an evil spirit in the house,—a small, selfish, envious, malicious spirit; people were cross, and they knew not why; felt injured, and they knew not why; the days were harder than those dreadful ones when fire and candle were never out, and every one was a watcher in the shadow of death.

As the season advanced, Julius took precisely the position which Stephen had foretold he would take. At first he deferred entirely to the squire; he received his orders, and then saw them carried out. Very soon he forgot to name the squire in the matter. He held consultations with the head man, and talked with him about the mowing and harvesting, and the sale of lambs and fleeces. The master's room was opened, and Julius sat at the table to receive tenants and laborers. In the squire's chair it was easy to feel that he was himself squire of Sandal-Side and Torver.

It was a most unhappy summer. Evils, like weeds, grow apace. There was scarcely any interval between some long-honored custom and its disappearance. To-day it was observed as it had been for a lifetime; the next week it had passed away, and appeared to be forgotten. "Such times I never saw," said Ann. "I have been at Sandal twenty-two years come Martinmas, but I'm going to Beverley next feast."

"You'll not do it, Ann. It's but talk."

"Nay, but I'm set on it. I have taken the 'fastening penny,' and I'm bound to make that good. Things are that trying here now, that I can't abide them longer."

All summer servants were going and coming at Seat-Sandal; the very foundations of its domestic life were broken up, and Charlotte's bright face had a constant wrinkle of worry and annoyance. Sophia was careful to point out the fact. "She has no housekeeping ability. Every thing is in a mess. If I only durst take hold of things. But Charlotte is such a spitfire, one

Amelia E. Barr

does not like to offer help. I would be only too glad to put things right, but I should give offence," etc. "The poison of asps under the tongue," and a very little of it, can paralyze and irritate a whole household.

Mowing-time and shearing-time and reaping-time came and went, but the gay pastoral festivals brought none of their old-time pleasure. The men in the fields did not like Julius in the squire's place, and they took no pains to hide the fact. Then he came home with complaints. "They were idle. They were disrespectful. The crops had fallen short." He could not understand it; and when he had expressed some dissatis-faction on the matter, the head man had told him, to take his grumbling to God Almighty. "An insolent race, these statesmen and Dale shepherds," he added; "if one of them owns ten acres, he thinks himself as good as if he owns a thousand."

"All well-born men, Julius, all of them; are they not, Charlotte? Eh? What?"

"So well born," answered Charlotte warmly, "that King James the First set up a claim to all these small estates, on the plea that their owners had never served a feudal lord, and were, therefore, tenants of the crown. But the large statesmen went with the small ones. They led them in a body to a heath between Kendal and Stavely, and there over two thousand men swore, 'that as they had their lands by the sword, they would keep them by the same.' So you see, Julius, they were gentlemen before the feudal system existed; they never put a finger under its authority, and they have long survived its fall."

"Well, for all that, they make poor servants."

"There's men that want Indian ryots or negro slaves to do

their turn. I want free men at Sandal-Side as long as I am squire of that name."

"They missed you sorely in the fields, father. It was not shearing-time, nor hay-time, nor harvest-time to any one in Sandal this year. But you will stand in your meadows again—God grant it!—next summer. And then how the men will work! And what shouting there will be at the sight of you! And what a harvest-home we shall have!"

And he caught her enthusiasm, and stood up to try his feet, and felt sure that he walked stronger, and would soon be down-stairs once more. And Julius, whose eyes love did not blind, felt a little scorn for those who could not see such evident decay and dissolution. "It is really criminal," he said to Sophia, "to encourage hopes so palpably false." For Julius, like all selfish persons, could perceive only one side of a question, the side that touched his own side. It never entered his mind that the squire was trying to cheer and encourage his wife and daughter, and was privately quite aware of his own condition. Sandal had not told him that he had received "the token," the secret message which every soul receives when the King desires his presence. He had never heard those solemn conversations which followed the reading of "The Evening Service," when the rector knelt by the side of his old friend, and they two talked with Death as with a companion. So, though Julius meddled much with Sandal affairs, there was a life there into which he never entered.

One evening in October, Charlotte was walking with Stephen. They had been to look at the new building, for every inch of progress was a matter of interest to them. As they came through the village, they perceived that Farmer Huet was holding his apple feast; for he was carrying from his house into his orchard a great bowl of spiced ale, and was followed by a merry company, singing wassail as they poured a little at the root of every tree:—

"Here's to thee, good apple-tree!
Whence thou may'st bud, and whence thou may'st blow,
Whence thou may'st bear apples enou';
Hats full, caps full,
Bushels full, sacks full.
Hurrah, then! Hurrah, then!
Here's to thee, good apple-tree!"

They waited a little to watch the procession round the orchard; and as they stood, Julius advanced from an opposite direction. He took a letter from his pocket, which he had evidently been to the mail to secure, for Charlotte watched him break the seal as he approached; and when he suddenly raised his head, and saw her look of amazement, he made a little bravado of the affair, and said, with an air of frankness, "It is a letter from Harry. I thought it was best for his letters not to come to the house. The mail-bag might be taken to the squire's room, and who knows what would happen if he should see one of these," and he tapped the letter significantly with his long pointed fore-finger.

"You should not have made such an arrangement as that, Julius, without speaking to mother. It was cruel to Harry. Why should the villagers think that the sight of a letter from him would be so dreadful to his own people?"

"I did it for the best, Charlotte. Of course, you will misjudge me."

"Ah! I know now why Polly Esthwaite called you, 'such a nice, kind, thoughtful gentleman as never was.' Is the letter for you?"

"Mr. Latrigg can examine the address if you wish."

"Mr. Latrigg distinctly refuses to look at the letter. Come, Charlotte, the air is cold and raw;" and with very scant courtesy they parted.

"What can it mean, Steve, Julius and Harry in correspondence? I don't know what to think of such a thing. Harry has only written once to me since he went away. There is something wrong in all this secrecy, you may depend upon it."

"I would not be suspicious, Charlotte. Harry is affectionate and trusting. Julius has written him letters full of sympathy and friendship; and the poor fellow, cut off from home and kindred, has been only too glad to answer. Perhaps we should have written also."

"But why did Julius take that trouble? Julius always has a motive for what he does. I mean a selfish motive. Has Harry written to you?"

"Only a few lines the very day he left. I have heard nothing since."

The circumstance troubled Charlotte far beyond its apparent importance. She could conceive of no possible reason for Julius interfering in Harry's life, and she had the feeling of a person facing a danger in the dark. Julius was also annoyed at her discovery. "It precipitates matters," he said to Sophia, "and is apparently an unlucky chance. But chance is destiny, and this last letter of Harry's indicates that all things are very nearly ready for me. As for your sister, Charlotte Sandal, I think she is the most interfering person I ever knew."

The air of the supper-table was one of reserve and offence. Only Sophia twittered and observed and wondered about all kinds of trivial things. "Mother has so many headaches now. Does she take proper care of herself, Charlotte? She ought to take exercise. Julius and I never neglect taking exercise. We think it a duty. No time do you say? Mother ought to take time. Poor, dear father was never unreasonable; he would wish mother to take time. What tasteless custards, Charlotte! I don't think Ann cares how she cooks now. When I was at home, and the eldest daughter, she always liked to have things nice. Julius, my dear one, can you find any thing fit to eat?" And so on, and so on, until Charlotte felt as if she must scream, or throw a plate down, or fly beyond the sight and sound of all things human.

The next evening Julius announced his intention of going abroad at once. "But I shall leave Sophia to be a little society for mother, and I shall not delay an hour beyond the time necessary for travel and business." He spoke with an air of conscious self-denial; and as Charlotte did not express any gratitude he continued, "Not that I expect any thanks, Sophia and I, but fortunately we find duty is its own reward."

"Are you going to see Harry?"

"I may do such a thing."

"Is he sick?"

"No."

"I hope he will not get sick while you are there." And then some passionate impulse took possession of her; her face glowed like a flame, and her eyes scintillated like sparks. "If any thing happens Harry while you are with him, I swear, by each separate Sandal that ever lived, that you shall account for it!"

"Oh, you know, Sophia dear, this is too much! Leave the table, my love. Your sister must be"—and he tapped his forehead; while Sophia, with a look of annihilating scorn, drew her drapery tight around her, and withdrew.

"What did I say? What do I think? What terror is in my heart? Oh, Harry, Harry, Harry!"

She buried her face in her hands, and sat lost in woeful thought,—sat so long that Phoebe the table-maid felt her delay to be unkind and aggravating; especially when one of the chamber-maids came down for her supper, and informed the rulers of the servants' hall that "Mrs. Julius was crying up-stairs about Miss Charlotte falling out with her husband."

"Mercy on us! What doings we have to bide with!" and Ann shook her check apron, and sat down with an air of nearly exhausted patience.

"You can't think what a taking Mr. Julius is in. He's going away to-morrow."

"For good and all?"

"Not he. He'll be back again. He has had a falling-out with Miss Charlotte."

"Poor lass! Say what you will, she has been hard set lately. I never knew nor heard tell of her being flighty and fratchy before the squire's trouble."

"Good hearts are plenty in good times, Ann Skelton. Miss Charlotte's temper is past all the last few weeks, she is that off-and-on and changeable like and spirity. Mrs. Julius says she does beat all."

"I don't pin my faith on what Mrs. Julius says. Not I."

In the east rooms the criticism was still more severe. Julius railed for an hour ere he finally decided that he never saw a more suspicious, unladylike, uncharitable, unchristianlike girl than Charlotte Sandal! "I am glad to get away from her a little while," he cried; "how can she be your sister, Sophia?"

So glad was he to get away, that he left before Charlotte came down in the morning. Ann made him a cup of coffee, and received a shilling and some suave words, and was quite sure after them that "Mr. Julius was the finest gentleman that ever trod in shoe-leather." And Julius was not above being gratified with the approbation and good wishes of servants; and it gave him pleasure to leave in the little hurrah of their bows and courtesies, their smiles and their good wishes.

He went without delay straight to the small Italian village in which Harry had made his home. Harry's letters had prepared him for trouble and poverty, but he had little idea of the real condition of the heir of Sandal-Side. A few bare rooms in some dilapidated palace, grim with faded magnificence, comfortless and dull, was the kind of place he expected. He found him in a small cottage surrounded by a barren, sandy patch of ground overgrown with neglected vines and vagabond weeds. The interior was hot and untidy. On a couch a woman in the firm grip of consumption was lying; an emaciated, feverish woman, fretful with acute suffering. A little child, wan and waxy-looking, and apparently as ill as its mother, wailed in a cot by her side. Signor Lanza was smoking under a fig-tree in the neglected acre, which had been a vineyard or a garden. Harry had gone into the village for some necessity; and when he returned Julius felt a shock and a pang of regret for the dashing young soldier squire that he had known as Harry Sandal.

He kissed his wife with passionate love and sorrow, and then turned to Julius with that mute look of inquiry which few find themselves able to resist.

"He is alive yet,—much better, he says; and Charlotte thinks he may be in the fields again next season."

"Thank God! My poor Beatrice and her baby! You see what is coming to them?"

"Yes."

"And I am so poor I cannot get her the change of air, the luxuries, the medicines, which would at least prolong life, and make death easy."

"Go back with me to Sandal-Side, and see the squire: he may listen to you now."

"Never more! It was cruel of father to take my marriage in such a way. He turned my life's joy into a crime, cursed every hour that was left me."

"People used to be so intense—'a few strong feelings,' as Mr. Wordsworth says—too strong for ordinary life. We really can't afford to love and hate and suffer in such a teetotal way now; but the squire came from the Middle Ages. This is a dreadfully hot place, Harry."

"Yes, it is. We were very much deceived in it. I bought it; and we dreamed of vineyards and milk and wine, and a long, happy, simple life together. Nothing has prospered with us. We were swindled in the house and land. The signor knows nothing about vines. He was born here, and wanted to come back and be a great man." And as he spoke he laughed hysterically, and took Julius into an inner room. "I don't want Beatrice to hear that I am out of money. She does not know I am destitute. That sorrow, at least, I have kept from her."

"Harry, I am going to make you a proposal. I want to be kind and just to you. I want to put you beyond the need of any one's help. Answer me one question truly. If your father dies, what will you do?"

"You said he was getting better. For God's sake, do not speak of his death."

"I am supposing a case. You would then be squire of Sandal-Side. Would you return there with Beatrice?"

"Ah, no! I know what those Dalesmen are. My father's feelings were only their feelings intensified by his relation to me. They would look upon me as my father's murderer, and Beatrice as an accessory to the deed."

"Still you would be squire of Sandal-Side."

"Mother would have to take my place, or Charlotte. I have thought of that. I could not bear to sit in father's chair, and go up and down the house. I should see him always. I should hear continually that awful cry with which he fell. It fills, even here, all the spaces of my memory and my dreams. I cannot go back to Sandal-Side. Nothing could take me back, not even my mother."

"Then listen, I am the heir failing you."

"No, no: there is my son Michael."

Julius was stunned for a moment. "Oh, yes! The child is a boy, then?"

"It is a boy. What were you going to say?"

"I was going to ask you to sell your rights to me for ten

thousand pounds. It would be better for you to have a sum like that in your hand at once, than to trust to dribbling remittances sent now and then by women in charge. You could invest that sum to noble purpose in America, become a citizen of the country, and found an American line, as my father has founded an Indian one."

"The poor little chap makes no difference. He is only born to die. And I think your offer is a good one. I am so worn out, and things are really desperate with me. I never can go back to England. I am sick to death of Florence. There are places where Beatrice might even yet recover. Yes, for her sake, I will sell you my inheritance. Can I have the money soon?"

"This hour. I had the proper paper drawn up before I came here. Read it over carefully. See if you think it fair and honorable. If you do, sign your name; and I will give you a check you can cash here in Florence. Then it will be your own fault if Beatrice wants change of air, luxuries, and medicine."

He laid the paper on the table, and Harry sat down and pretended to read it. But he did not understand any thing of the jargon. The words danced up and down. He could only see "Beatrice," "freedom from care," "power to get away from Florence," and the final thought, the one which removed his last scruple, "Lanza can have the cottage, and I shall be clear of him forever."

Without a word he went for a pen and ink, and wrote his name boldly to the deed of relinquishment. Then Julius handed him a check for ten thousand pounds, and went with him to the bank in order to facilitate the transfer of the sum to Harry's credit. On the street, in the hot sunshine, they stood a few minutes.

Amelia E. Barr

"You are quite satisfied, Harry?"

"You have saved me from despair. Perhaps you have saved Beatrice. I am grateful to you."

"Have I done justly and honorably by you?"

"I believe you have."

"Then good-by. I must hasten home. Sophia will be anxious, and one never knows what may happen."

"Julius, one moment. Tell my mother to pray for me. And the same word to Charlotte. Poor Charley! Sophia"—

"Sophia pities you very much, Harry. Sophia feels as I do. We don't expect people to cut their lives on a fifteenth-century pattern."

Then Harry lifted his hat, and walked away, with a shadow still of his old military, up-head manner. And Julius looked after him with contempt, and thought, "What a poor fellow he is! Not a word for himself, or a plea for that wretched little heir in his cradle. There are some miserable kinds of men in this world. I thank God I am not one of them!"

And the wretched Esau, with the ten thousand pounds in his pocket? Ah, God only knew his agony, his shame, his longing, and despair! He felt like an outcast. Yes, even when he clasped Beatrice in his arms, with promises of unstinted comforts; when she kissed him, with tender words and tears of joy,—he felt like an outcast.

CHAPTER X

THE NEW SQUIRE

"A word was brought,
Unto him,—the King himself desired his presence."

"The mystery of life
He probes; and in the battling din of things
That frets the feeble ear, he seeks and finds
A harmony that tunes the dissonant strife
To sweetest music."

This year the effort to keep Christmas in Seat-Sandal was a failure. Julius did not return in time for the festival, and the squire was unable to take any part in it. There had been one of those sudden, mysterious changes in his condition, marking a point in life from which every step is on the down-hill road to the grave. One day he had seemed even better than usual; the next morning he looked many years older. Lassitude of body and mind had seized the once eager, sympathetic man; he was weary of the struggle for life, and had *given up*. This change occurred just before Christmas; and Charlotte could not help feeling that the evergreens for the feast might, after all, be the evergreens for the funeral.

One snowy day between Christmas and New Year, Julius came home. Before he said a word to Sophia, she divined that he had succeeded in his object. He entered the house with the air of a master; and, when he heard how rapidly the squire was failing, he congratulated himself on his prudent alacrity in the matter. The next morning he was permitted an interview. "You have been a long time away, Julius," said the squire languidly, and without apparent interest in the subject.

"I have been a long journey."

"Ah! Where have you been? Eh?"

"To Italy."

The sick man flushed crimson, and his large, thin hands quivered slightly. Julius noted the change in him with some alarm; for, though it was not perhaps actually necessary to have the squire's signature to Harry's relinquishment, it would be more satisfactory to obtain it. He knew that neither Mrs. Sandal nor Charlotte would dispute Harry's deed; but he wished not only to possess Seat-Sandal, but also the good-will of the neighborhood, and for this purpose he must show a clear, clean right to the succession. He had explained the matter to Sophia, and been annoyed at her want of enthusiasm. She feared that any discussion relating to Harry might seriously excite and injure her father, and she could not bring herself to advise it. But the disapproval only made Julius more determined to carry out his own views; and therefore, when the squire asked, "Where have you been?" he told him the truth; and oh, how cruel the truth can sometimes be!

"I have been to Italy."

"To see"—

"Harry? Yes."

Then, without waiting to inform himself as to whether the squire wished the conversation dropped or continued, he added, "He was in a miserable condition,—destitute, with a dying wife and child."

"Child! Eh? What?"

"Yes, a son; a little chap, nothing but skin and bone and black eyes,—an Italian Sandal."

The squire was silent a few minutes; then he asked in a slow, constrained voice, "What did you do?"

"Harry sent for me in order that we might discuss a certain proposal he wished to make me. I have accepted it—reluctantly accepted it; but really it appeared the only way to help him to any purpose."

"What did Harry want? Eh? What?"

"He wanted to go to America, and begin a new life, and found a new house there; and, as he had determined never under any circumstances to visit Sandal-Side again, he asked me to give him the money necessary for emigration."

"Did you?"

"Yes, I did."

"For what? What equivalent could he give you?"

"He had nothing to give me but his right of succession. I

Amelia E. Barr

bought it for ten thousand pounds. A sum of money like that ought to give him a good start in America. I think, upon the whole, he was very wise."

"Harry Sandal sold my home and estate over my head, while I was still alive, without a word to me! God have mercy!"

"Uncle, he never thought of it in that light, I am sure."

"That is what he did; sold it without a thought as to what his mother's or sister's wishes might be. Sold it away from his own child. My God! The man is an immeasurable scoundrel; and, Julius Sandal, you are another."

"Sir?"

"Leave me. I am still master of Sandal. Leave me. Leave my house. Do not enter it again until my dead body has passed the gates."

"It will be right for you first to sign this paper."

"What paper? Eh? What?"

"The deed of Harry's relinquishment. He has my money. I look to your honor to secure me."

"You look the wrong road. I will sign no such paper,—no, not for twenty years of life."

He spoke sternly, but almost in a whisper. The strain upon him was terrible; he was using up the last remnants of his life to maintain it.

"That you should sign the deed is only bare honesty. I gave the money trusting to your honesty."

"I will not sign it. It would be a queer thing for me to be a partner in such a dirty job. The right of succession to Sandal, barring Harry Sandal, is not vested in you. It is in Harry's son. Whoever his mother may be, the little lad is heir of Sandal-Side; and I'll not be made a thief in my last hours by you. That's a trick beyond your power. Now, then, I'll waste no more words on you, good, bad, or indifferent."

He had, in fact, reached the limit of his powers, and Julius saw it; yet he did not hesitate to press his right to Sandal's signature by every argument he thought likely to avail. Sandal was as one that heard not, and fortunately Mrs. Sandal's entrance put an end to the painful interview.

This was a sorrow the squire had never contemplated, and it filled his heart with anxious misery. He strove to keep calm, to husband his strength, to devise some means of protecting his wife's rights. "I must send for Lawyer Moser: if there is any way out of this wrong, he will know the right way," he thought. But he had to rest a little ere he could give the necessary prompt instructions. Towards noon he revived, and asked eagerly for Stephen Latrigg. A messenger was at once sent to Up-Hill. He found Stephen in the barn, where the men were making the flails beat with a rhythm and regularity as exhilarating as music. Stephen left them at once; but, when he told Ducie what word had been brought him, he was startled at her look and manner.

"I have been looking for this news all day: I fear me, Steve, that the squire has come to 'the passing.' Last night I saw your grandfather."

"Dreamed of him?"

"Well, then, call it a dream. I saw your grandfather. He was in this room; he was sorting the papers he left; and, as I watched his hands, he lifted his head and looked at me. I have got my orders, I feel that. But wait not now, I will follow you anon."

In the "Seat" there was a distinct feeling of consummating calamity. The servants had come to a state of mind in which the expectation was rather a relief. They were only afraid the squire might rally again. In Mrs. Sandal's heart there was that resentful resignation which says to sorrow, "Do thy worst. I am no longer able to resist, or even to plead." Charlotte only clung to her dream of hope, and refused to be wakened from it. She was sure her father had been worse many a time. She was almost cross at Ducie's unusual visit.

About four o'clock Steve had a long interview with the squire. Charlotte walked restlessly to and fro in the corridor; she heard Steve's voice, strong and kind and solemn, and she divined what promises he was making to the dying man for herself and for her mother. But even her love did not anticipate their parting words,—

"Farewell, Stephen. Yet one word more. If Harry should come back—what of Harry? Eh? What?"

"I will stand by him. I will put my hand in his hand, and my foot with his foot. They that wrong Harry will wrong me, they that shame Harry will shame me. I will never call him less than a brother, as God hears me speak."

A light "that never was on sea or sky" shone in Sandal's fast dimming eyes, and irradiated his set gray countenance. "Stephen, tell him at death's door I turned back to forgive him—to bless him. I stretch—out—my hand—to—him."

At this moment Charlotte opened the door softly, and waved Stephen towards her. "Your mother is come, and she says she must see the squire." And then, before Stephen could answer, Ducie gently put them both aside. "Wait in the corridor, my children," she said: "none but God and Sandal must hear my farewell." With the words, she closed the door, and went to the dying man. He appeared to be unconscious; but she took his hand, stroked it kindly, and bending down whispered, "William, William Sandal! Do you know me?"

"Surely it is Ducie. It is growing dark. We must go home, Ducie. Eh? What?"

"William, try and understand what I say. You will go the happier to heaven for my words." And, as they grew slowly into the squire's apprehension, a look of amazement, of gratitude, of intense satisfaction, transfigured the clay for the last time. It seemed as if the departing soul stood still to listen. He was perfectly quiet until she ceased speaking; then, in a strange, unearthly tone, he uttered one word, "Happy." It was the last word that ever parted his lips. Between shores he lingered until the next daybreak, and then the loving watchers saw that the pallid wintry light fell on the dead. How peaceful was the large, worn face! How tranquil! How distant from them! How grandly, how terribly indifferent! To Squire William Sandal, all the noisy, sorrowful controversies of earth had grown suddenly silent.

The reading of the squire's will made public the real condition of affairs. Julius had spoken with the lawyer previously, and made clear to him his right in equity to stand in the heir's place. But the squires and statesmen of the Dales heard the substitution with muttered dissents, or in a silence still more emphatic of disapproval. Ducie and Mrs. Sandal and Charlotte were shocked and astounded at the revelation, and there was not a family in Sandal-Side who had that night a good word for Julius Sandal. He thought it very hard, and said so. He had not forced Harry in any way. He had taken no advantage of him. Harry was quite satisfied with the exchange, and what had other people to do with his affairs? He did not care for their opinion. "That for it!" and he snapped his fingers defiantly to every point of the compass. But, all the same, he walked the floor of the east rooms nearly all night, and kept Sophia awake to listen to his complaints.

Sophia was fretful and sleepy, and not as sympathetic with "the soul that halved her own," as centuries of fellow-feeling might have claimed; but she had her special worries. She perceived, even thus early, that as long as the late squire's widow was in the Seat, her own authority would be imperfect. "Of course, she did not wish to hurry her mother; but she would feel, in her place, how much more comfortable for all a change would be. And mother had her dower-house in the village; a very comfortable home, quite large enough for Charlotte and herself and a couple of maids, which was certainly all they needed."

Where did such thoughts and feelings spring from? Were they lying dormant in her heart that summer when the squire drove home his harvest, and her mother went joyfully up and down the sunny old rooms, always devising something for her girls' comfort or pleasures? In those days how proud Sophia had been of her father and mother! What indignation she would have felt had one suggested that the time was coming when she would be glad to see a stranger in her father's place, and feel impatient to say to her mother, "Step down lower; I would be mistress in your room"! Alas! there are depths in the human heart we fear to look into; for we know that often all that is necessary to assuage a great grief, or obliterate a great loss, is the inheritance of a fine mansion, or a little money, or a few jewels, or even a rich garment. And as soon as the squire was in his grave, Julius and Sophia began to discuss the plans which only a very shallow shame had made them reticent about before.

Indeed, it soon became necessary for others, also, to discuss the future. People soon grow unwelcome in a house that is not their own; and the new squire of Sandal-Side was eager to so renovate and change the place that it would cease to remind him of his immediate predecessors. The Sandals of past centuries were welcome, they gave dignity to his claims; but the last squire, and his son Harry Sandal, only reminded him of circumstances he felt it more comfortable to forget. So, during the long, dreary days of midwinter, he and Sophia occupied themselves very pleasantly in selecting styles of furniture, and colors of draperies, and in arranging for a full suite of Oriental rooms, which were to perpetuate in pottery and lacquerware, Indian bronzes and mattings, Chinese screens and cabinets, the Anglo-Indian possessor of the old Cumberland estate.

Even pending these alterations, others were in progress. Every family arrangement was changed in some respect. The hour for breakfast had been fixed at what Julius called a civilized time. This, of course, delayed every other meal; yet the servants, who had grumbled at over-work under the old authority, had not a complaint to make under the new. For the present master and mistress of Sandal were not people who cared for complaints. "If you can do the work, Ann, you may stay," said Sophia to the dissatisfied cook; "if not, the squire will pay you your due wages. He has a friend in London whose cook would like a situation in the country." After which explanation Ann behaved herself admirably, and never found her work hard, though dinner was two hours later, and the supper dishes were not sent in until eleven o'clock.

But, though Julius had succeeded in bringing his table so far within his own ideas of comfort, in other respects he felt his impotence to order events. Every meal-time brought him in contact with the widow Sandal and with Charlotte; and neither Sophia, nor yet himself, had felt able to request the late mistress to resign her seat at the foot of the table. And Sophia soon began to think it unkind of her mother not to see the position, and voluntarily amend it. "I do really think mother might have some consideration for me, Julius," she complained. "It puts me in such a very peculiar position not to take my place at my own table; and it is so trying and perplexing for the servants,—making them feel as if there were two mistresses."

"And always the calm, scornful face of your sister Charlotte at her side. Do you notice with what ostentatious obedience and attention she devotes herself to your mother?"

"She thinks that she is showing me my duty, Julius. But people have some duties toward themselves."

"And towards their husbands."

"Certainly. I thank Heaven I have always put my husband first." And she really glanced upwards with the complacent air of one who expected Heaven to imitate men, and "praise her for doing well unto herself."

"This state of things cannot go on much longer, Sophia."

"Certainly it cannot. Mother must look after her own house soon."

"I would speak to her to-day, Sophia. She has had six weeks now to arrange her plans, and next month I want to begin and put the house into decent condition. I think I will write to London this afternoon, and tell Jeffcott to send the polishers and painters on the 15th of March."

"Mother is so slow about things, I don't think she will be ready to move so early."

"Oh, I really can't stand them any longer! I can't indeed, Sophia, and I won't. I did not marry your mother and sister, nor yet buy them with the place. Your mother has her recognized rights in the estate, and she has a dower-house to which to retire; and the sooner she goes there now, the better. You may tell her I say so."

"You may as well tell her yourself, Julius."

"Do you wish me to be insulted by your sister Charlotte again? It is too bad to put me in such a position. I cannot punish two women, even for such shameful innuendos as I had to take when she sat at the head of the table. You ought to reflect, too, that the rooms they occupy are the best rooms in the house,—the master's rooms. I am going to have the oak walls polished, in order to bring out the carvings; and I think we will choose green and white for the carpets and curtains. The present furniture is dreadfully old-fashioned, and horribly full of old memories."

"Well, then, I shall give mother to understand that we expect to make these changes very soon."

"Depend upon it, the sooner your mother and Charlotte go to their own house, the better for all parties. For, if we do not insist upon it, they will stay and stay, until that Latrigg young man has his house finished. Then Charlotte will expect to be married from here, and we shall have all the trouble and expense of the affair. Oh, I tell you, Sophia, I see through the whole plan! But reckoning without me, and reckoning with me, are different things."

This conversation took place after a most unpleasant lunch.

Julius had come to it in a fretful, hypercritical mood. He had been calculating what his proposed changes would cost, and the sum total had given him a slight shock. He was like many extravagant people, subject to passing spells of almost contemptible economy; and at that hour the proposed future outlay of thousands did not trouble him so much as the actual penny-half-penny value of his mother-in-law's lunch.

He did not say so, but in some way the feeling permeated the table. The widow pushed her plate aside, and sipped her glass of wine in silence. Charlotte took a pettish pleasure in refusing what she felt she was unwelcome to. Both left the table before Julius and Sophia had finished their meal; and both, as soon as they reached their rooms, turned to each other with faces hot with indignation, and hearts angry with a sense of shameful unkindness.

Charlotte spoke first. "What is to be done, mother? I cannot see you insulted, meal after meal, in this way. Let us go at once. I have told you it would come to this. We ought to have moved immediately,—just as soon as Julius came here as master."

"My house in the village has been empty for three years. It is cold and damp. It needs attention of every kind. If we could only stay here until Stephen's house was finished: then you could be married."

"O mother dear, that is not possible! You know Steve and I cannot marry until father has been dead at least a year. It would be an insult to father to have a wedding in his mourning year."

"If your father knows any thing, Charlotte, he knows the trouble we are in. He would count it no insult."

"But all through the Dales it would be a shame to us. Steve and I would not like to begin life with the ill words or ill thoughts of our neighbors."

"What shall I do? Charlotte, dear, what shall I do?"

"Let us go to our own home. Better to brave a little damp and discomfort than constant humiliation."

"This is my home, my own dear home! It is full of memories of your father and Harry."

"O mother, I should think you would want to forget Harry!"

"No, no, no! I want to remember him every hour of the day and night. How could I pray for him, if I forgot him? Little you know how a mother loves, Charlotte. His father forgave him: shall I be less pitiful?—I, who nursed him at my breast, and carried him in my arms."

Charlotte did not answer. She was touched by her mother's fidelity, and she found in her own heart a feeling much akin to it. Their conversation reverted to their unhappy position, and to the difficulty of making an immediate change. For not only was the dower-house in an untenantable state, but the weather was very much against them. The gray weather, the gloomy sky, the monotonous rains, the melting snow, the spiteful east wind,—by all this enmity of the elements, as well as by the enmity in the household, the poor bereaved lady was saddened and controlled.

The wretched conversation was followed by a most unhappy silence. Both hearts were brooding over their slights and wrongs. Day by day Charlotte's life had grown harder to bear. Sophia's little flaunts and dissents, her astonishments and corrections, were almost as cruel as the open hatred of

Julius, his silence, his lowering brows, and insolence of proprietorship. To these things she had to add the intangible contempt of servants, and the feeling of constraint in the house where she had been the beloved child and the one in authority. Also she found the insolence which Stephen had to brave every time he called upon her just as difficult to bear as were her own peculiar slights. Julius had ceased to recognize him, had ceased to speak of him except as "that person." Every visit he made Charlotte was the occasion of some petty impertinence, some unmistakable assurance that his presence was offensive to the master of Seat-Sandal.

All these things troubled the mother also, but her bitterest pang was the cruelty of Sophia. A slow, silent process of alienation had been going on in the girl ever since her engagement to Julius: it had first touched her thoughts, then her feelings; now its blighting influence had deteriorated her whole nature. And in her mother's heart there were sad echoes of that bitter cry that comes down from age to age, "Oh, my son Absalom, Absalom! My son, my son!"

"O Sophia! oh, my child, my child! How can you treat me so? What have I done?" She was murmuring such words to herself when the door was opened, and Sophia entered. It was characteristic of the woman that she did not knock ere entering. She had always jealously guarded her rights to the solitude of her own room; and, even when she was a school-girl, it had been an understood household regulation that no one was to enter it without knocking. But now that she was mistress of all the rooms in Seat-Sandal, she ignored the simple courtesy towards others. Consequently, when she entered, she saw the tears in her mother's eyes. They only angered her. "Why should the sorrows of others darken her happy home?" Sophia was one of those women whom long regrets fatigue. As for her father, she reflected, "that he had been well nursed, decorously buried, and that every propriety had been attended to. It was, in her opinion, high time that the living—Julius and herself—should be thought of." The stated events of life—its regular meals, its trivial pleasures—had quite filled any void in her existence made by her father's death. If he had come back to earth, if some one had said to her, "He is here," she would have been far more embarrassed than delighted. The worldly advantages built upon the extinction of a great love! Sophia could contemplate them without a blush.

She came forward, shivering slightly, and stirred the fire. "How cold and dreary you are! Mother, why don't you cheer up and do something? It would be better for you than moping on the sofa."

"Suppose Julius had died six weeks ago, would you think of 'cheering up,' Sophia?"

"Charlotte, what a shameful thing to say!"

"Precisely what you have just said to mother."

"Supposing Julius dead! I never heard such a cruel thing. I dare say it would delight you."

"No, it would not; for Julius is not fit to die."

"Mother, I will not be insulted in my own house in such a way. Speak to Charlotte, or I must tell Julius."

"What have you come to say, Sophia?"

"I came to talk pleasantly, to see you, and"—

"You saw me an hour or two since, and were very rude and unkind. But if you regret it, my dear, it is forgiven."

"I do not know what there is to forgive. But really, Charlotte and you seem so completely unhappy and dissatisfied here, that I should think you would make a change."

"Do you mean that you wish me to go?"

"If you put words into my mouth."

"It is not worth while affecting either regret or offence, Sophia. How soon do you wish us to leave?"

The dowager mistress of Sandal-Side had stood up as she asked the question. She was quite calm, and her manner even cold and indifferent. "If you wish us to go to-day, it is still possible. I can walk as far as the rectory. For your father's sake, the rector will make us welcome.—Charlotte, my bonnet and cloak!"

"Mother! I think such threats very uncalled for. What will people say? And how can poor Julius defend himself against two ladies? I call it taking advantage of us."

"'Taking advantage?' Oh, no! Oh, no!—Charlotte, my dear, give me my cloak."

The little lady was not to be either frightened or entreated; and she deigned Julius—who had been hastily summoned by Sophia—no answer, either to his arguments or his apologies.

"It is enough," she cried, with a slight quiver in her voice, "it is enough! You turn me out of the home he gave me. Do you think that the dead see not? know not? You will find out, you will find out." And so, leaning upon Charlotte's arm, she walked slowly down the stairway, and into the dripping, soaking, gloomy afternoon. It was indeed wretched weather. A thick curtain of mist filled all the atmosphere, and made of daylight only a diluted darkness, in which it was hard to distinguish the skeletons of the trees which winter had stripped. The mountains had disappeared; there was no sky; a veil of chilling moisture and depressing gloom was over every thing. But neither Charlotte nor her mother was at that hour conscious of such inoffensive disagreeables. They were trembling with anger and sorrow. In a moment such a great event had happened, one utterly unconceived of, and unprepared for. Half an hour previous, the unhappy mother had dreaded the breaking away from her old life, and had declined to discuss with Charlotte any plan tending to such a consummation. Then, suddenly, she had taken a step more decided and unusual than had ever entered Charlotte's mind.

The footpath through the park was very wet and muddy. Every branch dropped water. They were a little frightened at what they were doing, and their hearts were troubled by many complex emotions. But fortunately the walk was a short one, and the shortest way to the rectory lay directly through the churchyard. Without a word Mrs. Sandal took it; and without a word she turned aside at a certain point, and through the long, rank, withered grasses walked straight to the squire's grave. It was yet quite bare; the snow had melted away, and it had a look as desolate as her own heart. She stood a few minutes speechless by its side; but the painfully tight clasp in which she held Charlotte's hand expressed better than any words could have done the tension of feeling, the passion of emotion, which dominated her. And Charlotte felt that silence was her mother's safety. If she spoke, she would weep, perhaps break down completely, and be unable to reach the shelter of the rectory.

The rector was walking about his study. He saw the two female forms passing through the misty graveyard, and up to his own front door; but that they were Mrs. Sandal and Charlotte Sandal, was a supposition beyond the range of his life's probabilities. So, when they entered his room, he was for the moment astounded; but how much more so, when Charlotte, seeing her mother unable to frame a word, said, "We have come to you for shelter and protection!"

Then Mrs. Sandal began to sob hysterically; and the rector called his housekeeper, and the best rooms were quickly opened and warmed, and the sorrowful, weary lady lay down to rest in their comfort and seclusion. Charlotte did not find their friend as unprepared for the event as she supposed likely. Private matters sift through the public mind in a way beyond all explanation, and "There had been a general impression," he said, "that the late squire's widow was very ill done to by the new squire."

Charlotte did not spare the new squire. All his petty ways of annoying her mother and herself and Stephen; all his small economies about their fire and food and comforts; all his scornful contempt for their household ways and traditions; all that she knew regarding his purchase of Harry's rights, and its ruthless revelation to her dying father,—all that she knew wrong of Julius, she told. It was a relief to do it. While he had been their guest, and afterwards while they had been his guests, her mouth had been closed. Week after week she had suffered in silence. The long-restrained tide of wrong flowed from her lips with a strange, pathetic eloquence; and, as the rector held her hands, his own were wet with her fast-falling tears. At last she laid her head against his shoulder, and wept as if her heart would break. "He has been our ruin," she cried, "our evil angel. He has used Harry's folly and father's goodness and Sophia's love—all of them—for his own selfish ends."

"He is a bad one. He should be hanged, and cheap at it! Hear him, talking of having lived so often! God have mercy! He is not worthy of one life, let alone of two."

At this juncture, Julius himself entered the room. Neither of its occupants had heard his arrival, and he saw Charlotte in the abandon of her grief and anger. She would have risen, but the rector would not let her. "Sit still, Charlotte," he said. "He has done his do, and you need not fear him any more. And dry your tears, my dearie; learn while you are young to squander nothing, not even grief." Then he turned to Julius, and gave him one of those looks which go through all disguises into the shoals and quicksands of the heart; such a look as that with which the tamer of wild beasts controls his captive.

"Well, squire, what want you?"

"I want justice, sir. I am come here to defend myself."

"Very well, I am here to listen."

Self-justification is a vigorous quality: Julius spoke with eloquence, and with a superficial show of right. The rector heard him patiently, offering no comment, and permitting no disputation. But, when Julius was finished, he answered with a certain stern warmth, "Say what you will, squire, you and I are of two ways of thinking. You are in the wrong, and you will be hard set to prove yourself in the right; and that is as true as gospel."

"I am, at least, a gentleman, rector; and I know how to treat gentlewomen."

"Gentle-man! Gentle-sinner, let me say! Will Satan care whether you be a peasant, or a star-and-garter gentleman? Tut, tut! in my office I know nothing about gentlemen. There are plenty of gentlemen with Beelzebub; and they will ring all eternity for a drop of water, and never find a servant to answer them."

"Sir, though you are a clergyman, you have no right to speak to me in such a manner."

"Because I am a clergyman, I have the right. If I see a man sleeping while the Devil rocks his cradle, have I not the right to say to him, 'Wake up, you are in danger'? Let me tell you, squire, you have committed more than one sin. Go home, and confess them to God and man. Above all, turn down a leaf in your Bible where a fool once asked, 'Who is my neighbor?' Keep it turned down, until you have answered the question better than you have been doing it lately."

"None of my neighbors can say wrong of me. I have always done my duty to them. I have paid every one what I owe"—

"Not enough, squire; not enough. Follow on, as Hosea says, to love them. Don't always give them the white, and keep the yolk for yourself. You know your duty. Haste you back home, then, and do it."

"I will not be put off in such a way, sir. You must interfere in this matter: make these silly women behave themselves. I cannot have the whole country-side talking of my affairs."

"Me interfere! No, no! I am not in your livery, squire; and I won't fight your quarrels. Sir, my time is engaged."

"I have a right"—

"My time is engaged. It is my hour for reading the Evening Service. Stay and hear it, if you desire. But it is a bad neighborhood, where a man can't say his prayers quietly." And he stood up, walked slowly to his reading-desk, and began to turn the leaves of the Book of Common Prayer.

Then Julius went out in a passion, and the rector muttered,

"The Devil may quote Scripture, but he does not like to hear it read. Come, Charlotte, let us thank God, thank him twice, nay, thrice, not alone for the faith of Christ Jesus, but also for the legacy of Christ Jesus. Oh, child, amid earth's weary restlessness and noisy quarrels, how rich a legacy,"—

"'Peace I leave with you. My peace I give unto you.'"

CHAPTER XI

SANDAL AND SANDAL

"Time will discover every thing; it is a babbler, and speaks even when no question is put."

"Run, spindles! Run, and weave the threads of doom."

Next morning very early, Stephen had a letter from Charlotte. He was sitting at breakfast with Ducie when the rector's boy brought it; and it came, as great events generally come, without any premonition or heralding circumstance. Ducie was pouring out coffee; and she went on with her employment, thinking, not of the letter Stephen was opening, but of the malt, and of the condition of the brewing-boiler. An angry exclamation from Stephen made her lift her eyes to his face. "My word, Stephen, you are put out! What's to do?"

"Julius has turned Mrs. Sandal and Charlotte from house and home, yesterday afternoon. They are at the rectory. I am going, mother."

"Stop a moment, Steve. This is now my affair."

Stephen looked at his mother with amazement. Her

countenance, her voice, her whole manner, had suddenly changed. An expression of angry purpose was in her wide-open eyes and firm mouth, as she asked, "Can you or Jamie, or any of the men, drive me to Kendal?"

"To-day?"

"I want to leave within an hour."

"The rain down-pours; and it is like to be worse yet, if the wind does not change."

"If it were ten times worse, I must to Kendal. I am much to blame that I have let weather stop me so far and so long. While Dame Nature was busy about her affairs, I should have been minding mine. Deary me, deary me!"

"If you are for Kendal, then I will drive. The cart-road down the fell is too bad to trust you with any one but myself. Can we stop a moment at the rectory on our road?"

"We can stop a goodish bit. I have a deal to say to the parson. Have the tax-cart ready in half an hour; for there will be no betterness in the weather until the moon—God bless her!—is full round; and things are past waiting for now."

In twenty minutes Ducie was ready. The large cloak and hood of the Daleswoman wrapped her close. She was almost indistinguishable in its folds. The rector met her with a little irritation. It was very early to be disturbed, and he thought her visit would refer, doubtless, to some trivial right between her son and Charlotte Sandal; besides which, he had made up his mind to discuss the Sandal affairs with no one.

But Ducie had spoken but a few moments before a remarkable change took place in his manner. He was bending eagerly forward, listening to her half-whispered words with the greatest interest and amazement. As she proceeded, he could scarcely control his emotion; and very soon all other expressions were lost in one of a satisfaction that was almost triumph.

"I will keep them here until you return," he answered; "but let me tell you, Ducie, you have been less quick to do right than I thought of you."

"The fell has been a hard walk for an old woman, the cart-road nearly impassable until this rain washed away the drifts; but I did not neglect my duty altogether, neither, parson. Moser was written to six weeks since, and he has been at work. Maybe, after all, no time has been lost. I'll away now, if you will call Stephen. Don't let Mrs. Sandal 'take on' more than you can help;" and, as Stephen lifted the reins, "You think it best to bring all here?"

"Far away best. God speed you!" He watched them out of sight,—his snowy hair and strong face and black garments making a vivid picture in the misty, drippy doorway,—and then, returning to his study, he began his daily walk up and down its carpeted length, with a singularly solemn elation. Ere long, the thoughtful stride was accompanied by low, musical mutterings, dropping from his lips in such majestic cadences that his steps involuntarily fell to their music in a march-like rhythm.

"Daughter of Justice, wronged Nemesis,
Thou of the awful eyes,
Whose silent sentence judgeth mortal life,—
Thou with the curb of steel,
Which proudest jaws must feel,
Stayest the snort and champ of human strife.

Under thy wheel unresting, trackless, all
Our joys and griefs befall;
In thy full sight our secret things go on;
Step after step, thy wrath
Follows the caitiff's path,
And in his triumph breaks his vile neck bone.
To all alike, thou meetest out their due,
Cubit for cubit, inch for inch,—stern, true."

At the word "true" he paused a moment, and touched with his finger an old black volume on one of the book-shelves. "'Stern, true,' whether Euripides says 'cubit for cubit,' or Moses 'an eye for an eye,' or Solomon that 'he that troubleth his own house shall inherit the wind.' Stern, true; for surely that which a man sows he shall also reap."

After a while he went up-stairs and talked with Mrs. Sandal and Charlotte. They were much depressed and very anxious, and had what Charlotte defined "a homeless feeling." "But you must be biddable, Charlotte," said the rector; "you must remain here until Stephen returns. Ducie had business that could not wait, and who but Stephen should drive her? When he comes back, we will all look to it. You shall not be very long out of your own home; and, in the mean time, how welcome you are here!"

"It seems such a weary time, sir; so many months that we have been in trouble."

"It was all night long, once, with some tired, fearful ones 'toiling in rowing;' but in the fourth watch came Christ and help to them. It is nigh hand—the 'fourth watch'—with you; so be cheerful."

Yet it was the evening of the sixth day before Ducie and Stephen returned. It was still raining heavily, and Ducie only waited a moment or two at the rectory gate. Charlotte was amazed to see the old clergyman hasten through the plashing shower to speak to her. "Surely Ducie's business must have a great deal of interest to the rector, mother: he has gone out to speak to her, and such weather too."

"Ducie was always a favorite with him. I hope, now that her affairs have been attended to, ours may receive some care."

Charlotte answered only by a look of sympathy. It had seemed to her a little hard that their urgent need must wait upon Ducie's business; that Stephen should altogether leave them in their extremity; that her anxious inquiries and suggestions, her plans and efforts about their new home, should have been so coldly received, and so positively put aside until Ducie and Stephen came back. And she had a pang of jealousy when she saw the rector, usually so careful of his health, hasten with slippered feet and uncovered head, through the wet, chilling atmosphere, to speak to them.

He came back with a radiant face, however, and Charlotte could hear him moving about his study; now rolling out a grand march of musical Greek syllables from Homer or Euripides, anon breaking into some familiar verse of Christian song. And, when tea was served, he went up-stairs for the ladies, and escorted them to the table with a manner so beaming and so happily predictive that Charlotte could not but catch some of its hopeful spirit.

Just as they sat down to the tea-table, the wet, weary travellers reached Up-Hill. With a sigh of pleasure and content, Ducie once more passed into its comfortable shelter; and never had it seemed to her such a haven of earthly peace. Her usually placid face bore marks of strong emotion; she was physically tired; and Stephen was glad to see her among the white fleeces of his grandfather's big chair, with her feet outstretched to the blazing warmth of the fire, and their cosey tea-service by her side. Always reticent with him, she had been very tryingly so on their journey. No explanation of it had been given; and he had been permitted to pass his time among the looms in Ireland's mill, while she and the lawyer were occupied about affairs to which even his signature was not asked.

As they sat together in the evening, she caught his glance searching her face tenderly; and she bent forward, and said, "Kiss me, Stephen, my dear lad. I have seen this week how kind and patient, how honorable and trustful, thou art. Well, then, the hour has come that will try thy love to the uttermost. But wise or unwise, all that has been done has been done with good intent, and I look for no word to pain me from thy mouth. Stephen, what is thy name?"

"Stephen Latrigg."

"Nay, but it isn't."

Stephen blushed vividly; his mother's face was white and calm. "I would rather be called Latrigg than—the other name, than by my father's name."

"Has any one named thy father to thee?"

"Charlotte told me what you and she said on the matter. She understood his name to be Pattison. We were wondering if our marriage could be under my adopted name, that was all, and things like it."

Ducie was watching his handsome face as he spoke, and feeling keenly the eager deprecation of pain to herself, mingling with the natural curiosity about his own identity, which the cloud upon his early years warranted. She looked at him steadily, with eyes shining brightly through tears.

"Your name is not Pattison, neither is it Latrigg. When you marry Charlotte Sandal, it must be by your own true name; and that is Stephen Sandal."

"Stephen Sandal, mother?"

"Yes. You are the son of Launcelot Sandal, the late squire's eldest brother."

"Then, mother, then I am—What am I, mother?"

"You are squire of Sandal-Side and Torver. No living man but you has a right to the name, or the land, or to Seat-Sandal."

"I should have known this before, mother."

"I think not. We had, father and I, what we believed good reasons, and kind reasons, for holding our peace. But times and circumstances have changed; and, where silence was once true friendship and kindness, it is now wrong and cruelty. Many years ago, Stephen, when I was young and beautiful, Launcelot Sandal loved me. And my father and Launcelot's father loved each other as David and Jonathan loved. They were scarcely happy apart; and not even to please the proud mistress Charlotte, would the squire loosen the grip of heart and hand between them. But your father was more under his mother's influence: proud lad as he was, he feared her; and when she discovered his love for me, there was such a scene between them as no man will go through twice in his lifetime. I have no excuse to make for marrying him secretly except the old, old one, Stephen. I loved him, loved him as women have loved, and will love, from the beginning to the end of time."

"Dear mother, there was no wrong in that. But why did you let the world think you loved a man beneath you? an uneducated shepherd like my reputed father? That wronged not only you, but those behind and those after you."

"We were afraid of many things, and we wished to spare the friendship between our fathers. There were many other reasons, scarcely worth repeating now."

"And what became of the shepherd?"

"He was not Cumberland born. He came from the Cheviot Hills, and was always fretting for the border life: so he gladly fell in with the proposal your father made him. One summer morning he said he was going to herd the lambs on Latrigg Fell, but he went to Egremont. Your father had gone there a week before; but he came back that night, and met me at Ravenglass. We were married in Egremont church, by Parson Sellafield, and went to Whitehaven, where we lived quietly and happily for many a week. Pattison witnessed our marriage, and then, with gold in his pocket, took the border road. He went to Moffat and wed the girl he loved, and has been shepherding on Loch Fell ever since."

"He is alive, then?"

"He is at the Salutation Inn at Ambleside to-night. So, also, is Parson Sellafield, and the man and woman with whom we staid in Whitehaven, and in whose house you were born and lived until your fourth year. They are called Chisholm, and have been at Up-Hill many times."

"I remember them."

"And I did not intend that they should forget you."

"I have always heard that Launcelot Sandal was drowned."

"You have always heard that your father was drowned? That was near by the truth. While in Whitehaven, he wrote to his brother Tom, who was living and doing well in India. When his answer came, we determined to go to Calcutta; but I was not in a state of health fit for such a journey as that then was. So it was decided that your father should go first, and get a home ready for me. He left in the 'Lady Liddel,' and she was lost at sea. Your father was in an open boat for many days, and died of exhaustion."

"Who told you so, mother?"

"The captain lived to reach his home again, and he brought me his watch and ring and last message. He never saw your face, my lad, he never saw your face."

A silence of some minutes ensued. Ducie had long ceased to weep for her dead love, but he was unforgotten. Her silence was not oblivion: it was a sanctuary where lights were burning round the shrine, over which the wings of affection were folded.

"When my father was gone, then you came back to Up-Hill?"

"No: I did not come back until you were in your fourth year. Then my mother died, and I brought you home. At the first moment you went straight to your grandfather's heart; and that night, as you lay asleep upon his knee, I told him the truth, as I tell it to you this night. And he said to me, 'Ducie, things have settled a bit lately. The squire has got over his trouble about Launcie; and young William is the acknowledged heir, and the welcome heir. He is going to marry Alice Morecombe at the long last, but it will make a big difference if Launcelot's son steps in where nobody wants him. Now, then,' he said, 'I will tell thee a far better way. We will give this dear lad my own name, none better in old Cumbria; and we will save gold, and we will make gold, to put it to the very front in the new times that are coming. And he will keep my name on the face of the earth, and so please the great company of his kin behind him. And it will be far better for him to be the top-sheaf of the Latriggs, than to force his way into Seat-Sandal, where there is neither love nor welcome for him.'"

"And I thought the same thing, Stephen; and after that, our one care was to make you happy, and to do well to you. That you were a born Sandal, was a great joy to him, for he loved your father and your grandfather; and, when Harry came, he loved him also, and he liked well to see you two on the fells together. Often he called me to come and look at you going off with your rods or guns; and often he said, 'Both fine lads, Ducie, but our Steve is the finer.'"

"Oh, mother, I cannot take Harry's place! I love Harry, and I did not know how much until this hour"—

"Stop a bit, Stephen. When Harry grew up, and went into the army, your grandfather wasn't so satisfied with what he had done. 'Here's a fine property going to sharpers and tailors and Italian singing-women,' he used to say; and he felt baddish about it. And yet he loved Squire William, as he had loved his father, and Mistress Alice and Harry and Sophia and Charlotte; why, he thought of them like his own flesh and blood. And he could not bear to undo his kindness. And he could not bear to tell Squire William the truth, for he knew well that he would undo it. So one day he sent for Lawyer Moser; and the two of them together found out a plan that seemed fair, for both Sandal and Latrigg.

"You were to remain Stephen Latrigg, unless it was to ward off wrong or ruin in Sandal-Side. But if ever the day came when Sandal needed Latrigg, you were to claim your right, and stand up for Sandal. Such a state of things as Harry brought about, my father never dreamed of. He would not have been able to think of a man selling away his right to a place like Seat-Sandal; and among all the villains he ever knew, or heard tell of, he couldn't have picked out one to lead him to such a villain as Julius Sandal. So, you see, he left no special directions for such a case, and I was a bit feared to move in too big a hurry; and, maybe, I was a bit of a coward about setting every tongue in Sandal-Side talking about me and my bygone days.

"But, when the squire died, I thought from what Charlotte told me of the Julius Sandals, that there would have to be a change; and when I saw your grandfather sorting the papers for me, and heard that Mistress Alice and Charlotte had been forced to leave their home, I knew that the hour for the change had struck, and that I must be about the business. Moser was written to soon after the funeral of Squire William. He has now all the necessary witnesses and papers ready. He is at Ambleside with them, and to-morrow morning they will have a talk with Mr. Julius at Seat-Sandal."

"I wonder where Harry Sandal is."

"After you, comes Harry. Your grandfather did not forget him. There is a provision in the will, which directs, that if, for any cause not conceivable by the testator, Harry Sandal must resign in favor of Stephen Sandal, then the land and money devised to you, as his heir, shall become the property of Harry Sandal. In a great measure you would only change places, and that is not a very hard punishment for a man who cared so little for his family home as Harry did. So you see,

Stephen, you must claim your rights in order to give Harry his."

The facts of this conversation opened up endlessly to the mother and son, and hour after hour it was continued without any loss of interest. But the keenest pleasure his new prospects gave Stephen referred itself to Mrs. Sandal and Charlotte. He could now reinstate them in their old home and in their old authority in it. For the bright visions underneath his eyelids, he could not sleep,—visions of satisfied affection, and of grief and humiliation crowned with joy and happiness and honor.

It had been decided that Stephen should drive his mother to the rectory in the morning, and there they were to wait the result of Moser's interview with Julius. The dawning came up with sunshine; the storm was over, the earth lay smiling in that "clear shining after rain," which is so exhilarating and full of promise. The sky was as blue, the air as fresh, fell and wood, meadow and mountain, as clean and bright as if they had just come new from the fingers of the Almighty. Ducie was handsomely dressed in dark violet-colored satin, and Stephen noticed with pride how well her rich clothing and quiet, dignified manner became her; while Ducie felt even a greater pride in the stately, handsome young man who drove her with such loving care down Latrigg fell that eventful morning.

Julius was at breakfast when the company from Ambleside were shown into the master's room in Seat-Sandal. The lawyer sent in his card; and Julius, who knew him well, was a trifle annoyed by the visit. "It will be about your mother's income, Sophia," he said, as he viciously broke the egg he was holding; "now mind, I am not going to yield one inch."

"Why should you, Julius? I am sure we have been blamed

and talked over enough. We never can be popular here."

"We don't want to be popular here. When we have refurnished the house, we will bring our company from Oxford and London and elsewhere. We will have fine dinners and balls, hunting-parties and fishing-parties; and, depend upon it, we shall very soon have these shepherd lords and gentlemen begging for our favor."

"Oh, you don't know them, Julius! They would not break bread with us if they were starving."

"Very well. What do I care?"

But he did care. When the wagoners driving their long teams pretended not to hear his greeting, for the jingling of their bells, he knew it was pretence, and the wagoners' aversion hurt him. When the herdsmen sauntered away from his path, and preferred not to talk to him, he felt the bitterness of their dislike, though they were only shepherds. When the gentlemen of the neighborhood looked straight before them, and did not see him in their path, he burned with an indignation he would have liked well to express. But no one took the trouble to offend him by word or deed, and a man cannot pick a quarrel with people for simply letting him alone.

Sophia's opinion recalled one or two of these events that were particularly galling; and he finished his breakfast in a sulky, leisurely fashion, to such reflections as they evoked. Then, with a cigar in his mouth, he went to the master's room to see Moser. He had been told that other parties were there also, but he did not surmise that their business was identical. Yet he noticed the clergyman on entering, and appeared inclined to attend to his request first; but as he courteously waved his claim away, and retired to the other end of the room, Julius said curtly,—

"Well, Mr. Moser, good-morning, sir."

The lawyer was pretending to be absorbed in the captions of the papers in his hand, for he was offended at being kept waiting so long: "As if a bite of victuals was of more ado than business that could bring Matthew Moser all the road from Kendal."

"Good-morning, Mr. Sandal."

The omission of "Squire," and the substitution of "Mr.," annoyed Julius very much, though he had not a suspicion of the lawyer's errand; and he corrected the mistake with a bland smile on his lips, and an angry light in his eyes. Moser, in reply, selected one particular paper, and put it into the hand of Julius.

"Acting for Squire Sandal, I would be a middling bad sort of a lawyer to give you his name. Eh?"

"You are talking in riddles, sir."

"Eh! But I always read my riddles, Mr. Sandal. I am here to take possession of house and land, for the real heir of Sandal-Side."

"I bought his right, as you know very well. You have Harry Sandal's own acknowledgment."

"Eh? But you see, Harry Sandal never had a penny-worth of right to sell. Launcelot Sandal left a son, and for him I am acting. Eh?"

"Launcelot Sandal was drowned. He never married."

"Eh, but he did!—Parson Sellafield, what do you say

about that?"

"I married him on July 11, 18—, at Egremont church. There," pointing to Matt Pattison, "is the witness. Here is a copy of the license and the 'lines.' They are signed, 'Launcelot Sandal' and 'Ducie Latrigg.'"

"Confusion!"

"Eh? No, no! There's not a bit of confusion, Mr. Sandal. It is all as clear as the multiplication table, and there is nothing clearer than that. Launcelot Sandal married Ducie Latrigg; they had one son, Stephen Sandal, otherwise known as Stephen Latrigg: proofs all ready, sir, not a link missing, Mr. Sandal. When will you vacate? The squire is inclined to be easy with you, and not to back-reckon, unless you force him to do so."

"This is a conspiracy, Moser."

"Conspiracy! Eh? Ugly word, Mr. Sandal. An actionable word, I may say."

"It is a conspiracy. You shall hear from me through some respectable lawyer."

"In the mean time, Mr. Sandal, I have taken, as you will see, the proper legal steps to prevent you wasting any more of the Sandal revenues. Every shilling you touch now, you will be held responsible for. Also," and he laid another paper down, "you are hereby restrained from removing, injuring, or in any way changing, or disposing of, the present furniture of the Seat. The squire insists specially on this direction, and he kindly allows you seven days to remove your private effects. A very reasonable gentleman is Squire Sandal."

Without further courtesies they parted; and the deposed squire locked the room-door, lifted the various documents, and read them with every sense he had. Then he went to Sophia; and at that hour he was almost angry with her, although he could not have told how, or why, such a feeling existed. When he opened the door of the parlor, her first words were a worry over the non-arrival, by mail, of some floss-silks, needful in the bird's-nest she was working for a fire-screen.

"They have not come, Julius," she cried, with a face full of inquiry and annoyance.

"They? Who?"

"The flosses for my bird's-nest. The eggs must be in white floss."

"The bird's nest can go to Jericho, or Calcutta, or into the fire. We are ordered to leave Seat-Sandal in seven days."

"I would not be so absurd, Julius, so unfeeling, so ungentlemanly."

"Well, then, my soul," and he bowed with elaborate grace, "Stephen Latrigg, squire of Sandal-Side, orders us to leave in seven days. Can you be ready?"

She looked into the suave, mocking, inscrutable face, shrugged her shoulders, and began to count her stitches. Julius had many varieties of ill-humor. She regarded this statement only as a new phase of his temper; but he soon undeceived her. With a pitiless exactness he went over his position, and, in doing so, made the hopelessness of his case as clear to himself as it was to others. And yet he was determined not to yield without a struggle; though, apart from the income of Sandal, which he could not reach, he had little money and no credit.

The story, with all its romance of attachment and its long trial of faithful secrecy, touched the prejudices and the sympathies of every squire and shepherd between Duddon and Esk and Windermere. Stephen came to his own, and they received him with open arms. But for Julius, there was not a "seat" in the Dales, nor a cottage on the fells, no, nor a chair in any of the local inns, where he was welcome. He stood his social excommunication longer than could have been expected; and, even at the end, his surrender was forced from him by the want of money, and the never-ceasing laments of Sophia. She was clever enough to understand from the first, that fighting the case was simply "indulging Julius in his temper;" and she did not see the wisdom of spending what little money they had in such a gratification.

"You have been caught in your own trap, Julius," she said aggravatingly. "Very clever people often are. It is folly to struggle. You had better ask Stephen to pay you back the ten thousand pounds. I think he ought to do that. It is only common honesty."

But Stephen had not the same idea of common honesty as Sophia had. He referred Julius to Harry.

"Harry, indeed! Harry who is in New York making ducks and drakes of your money, Julius,—trying to buy shares and things that he knows no more of than he knows of Greek. It's a shame!" and Sophia burst into some genuine tears over the reflection.

Still the idea, on a less extravagant basis, seemed possible to Steve. He began to think that it would be better to compromise matters with the Julius Sandals; better to lose a thousand pounds, or even two thousand pounds, if, by doing so, he could at once restore Mrs. Sandal and Charlotte to their home. And he was on the point of making a proposition of this kind, when it was discovered that Julius and his wife had silently taken their departure.

"It is a hopeless fight against destiny," said Julius. "When the purse is empty, any cause is weak. I have barely money to take us to Calcutta, Sophia. It is very disagreeable to go there, of course; but my father advised this step, and I shall remind him of it. He ought, therefore, to re-arrange my future. It is hard enough for me to have lost so much time carrying out his plans. And I should write a letter to your mother before you go, if I were you, Sophia. It is your duty. She ought to have her cruel behavior to you pointed out to her."

Sophia did her duty. She wrote a very clever letter, which really did make both her mother and sister wretchedly uncomfortable. Charlotte held it in her hand with a heart-ache, wondering whether she had indeed been as envious and unjust and unkind as Sophia felt her to have been; and Mrs. Sandal buried her face in her sofa pillow, and had a cry over her supposed partiality and want of true motherly feeling. "They had been so misunderstood, Julius and she,—wilfully misunderstood, she feared; and they were being driven to a foreign land, a deadly foreign land, because Charlotte and Stephen had raised against them a social hatred they had not the heart to conquer. If they defended themselves, they must accuse those of their own blood and house, and they were not mean enough to do such a thing as that. Oh, no! Sophia Sandal had always done her duty, and always would do it forever." And broad statements are such confusing, confounding things, that for one miserable hour the mother and sister felt as mean and remorseful as Sophia and Julius could desire. Then the rector read the letter aloud, and dived down into its depths as if it was a knotty text, and showed the two simple women on what false conditions all of its accusations rested.

At the same time Julius wrote a letter also. It was to Harry Sandal,—a very short letter, but destined to cause nearly six years of lonely, wretched wandering and anxious sorrow.

DEAR HARRY,—There is great trouble about that ten thousand pounds. It seems you had no right to sell. "Money on false pretences," I think they call it. I should go West, far West, if I were you.

Your friend,

JULIUS SANDAL.

He read it to Sophia, and she said, "What folly! Let Harry return home. You have heard that he comes into the Latrigg money. Very well, let him come home, and then you can make him pay you back. Harry is very honorable."

"There is not the slightest chance of Harry paying me back. If he had a million, he wouldn't pay me back. Harry spoke me fair, but I caught one look which let me see into his soul. He hated me for buying his right. With my money in his hand, he hated me. He would toss his hat to the stars if he heard how far I have been over-reached. Next to Charlotte Sandal, I hate Harry Sandal; and I am going to send him a road that he is not likely to return. I don't intend Stephen and Harry to sit together, and chuckle over me. Besides, your mother and Charlotte are surely calculating upon having 'dear Harry' and 'poor Harry' at home again very soon. I have no doubt Charlotte is planning about that Emily Beverley already. For Harry is to have Latrigg Hall when it is finished, I hear."

"Really? Is that so? Are you sure?"

"Harry is to have the new hall, and all of old Latrigg's gold and property."

"Julius, would it not be better to try and get around Harry? We could stay with him. I cannot endure Calcutta, and I always did like Harry."

"And I always detested him. And he always detested me. No, my sweet Sophia, there is really nothing for us but a decent lodging-house on the shady side of the Chowringhee Road. My father can give me a post in 'The Company,' and I must get as many of its rupees as I can manage. Go through the old rooms, and bid them farewell, my soul. We shall not come back to Seat-Sandal again in this chapter of our eternity." And with a mocking laugh he turned away to make his own preparations.

"But why go in the night, Julius? You said to-night at eleven o'clock. Why not wait until morning?"

"Because, beloved, I owe a great deal of money in the neighborhood. Stephen can pay it for me. I have sent him word to do so. Why should we waste our money? We have done with these boors. What they think of us, what they say of us, shall we mind it, my soul, when we drive under the peopuls and tamarinds at Barrackpore, or jostle the crowds upon the Moydana, or sit under the great stars and listen to the tread of the chokedars? All fate, Sophia! All fate, soul of my soul! What is Sandal-Side? Nothing. What is Calcutta? Nothing. What is life itself, my own one? Only a little piece out of something that was before, and will be after."

* * * * *

Who that has seen the Cumberland moors and fells in July can ever forget them?—the yellow broom and purple heather, the pink and white waxen balls of the rare vacciniums, the red-leaved sundew, the asphodels, the cranberries and blueberries and bilberries, and the wonderful green mosses in all the wetter places; and, above and around all, the great mountain chains veiled in pale, ethereal atmosphere, and rising in it as airy and unsubstantial as if they could tremble in unison with every thrill of the ether above them.

It was thus they looked, and thus the fells and the moors looked, one day in July, eighteen months after the death of Squire William Sandal,—his daughter Charlotte's wedding-day. From far and near, the shepherd boys and lasses were travelling down the craggy ways, making all the valleys ring to their wild and simple songs, and ever and anon the bells rung out in joyful peals; and from Up-Hill to Seat-Sandal, and around the valley to Latrigg Hall, there were happy companies telling each other, "Oh, how beautiful was the bride with her golden hair flowing down over her dress of shining white satin!" "And how proud and handsome the bridegroom!" "And how lovely in their autumn days the two mothers! Mistress Alice Sandal leaning so confidently upon the arm of the stately Mrs. Ducie Sandal." "And how glad was the good rector!" Little work, either in field or house or fellside, was done that day; for, when all has been said about human selfishness, this truth abides,—in the main, we do rejoice with those who rejoice, and we do weep with those who weep.

The old Seat was almost gay in the sunshine, all its windows open for the wandering breezes, and its great hall doors set wide for the feet of the new squire and his bride. For they were too wise to begin their married life by going away from their home; they felt that it was better to come to it with the bridal benediction in their ears, and the sunshine of the wedding-day upon their faces.

The ceremony had been delayed some months, for Stephen had been in America seeking Harry; seeking him in the great cities and in the lonely mining-camps, but never coming upon his foot steps until they had been worn away into forgetfulness. At last the rector wrote to him, "Return home, Stephen. We are both wrong. It is not human love, but God love, that must seek the lost ones. If you found Harry now, and brought him back, it would be too soon. When his lesson is learned, the heart of God will be touched, and he will say, 'That will do, my son. Arise, and go home.'"

And when Mrs. Sandal smiled through her tears, for the hope's sake, he took her hand, and added solemnly, "Be confident and glad, you shall see Harry come joyfully to his own home. Oh, if you could only listen, angels still talk with men! Raphael, the affable angel, loves to bring them confidences. God also speaks to his children in dreams, and by the oracles that wait in darkness. If we know not, it is because we ask not. But I know, and am sure, that Harry will return in joy and in peace. And if the dead look over the golden bar of heaven upon their earthly homes, Barf Latrigg, seeing the prosperity of the two houses, which stand upon his love and his self-denial, will say once more to his friend, 'William, I did well to Sandal.'"

Other books by this author

The Bow of Orange Ribbon

The Maid of Maiden Lane

The Man Between

A Knight of the Nets

Choose from Thousands of 1stWorldLibrary Classics By

A. M. Barnard
Ada Leverson
Adolphus William Ward
Aesop
Agatha Christie
Alexander Aaronsohn
Alexander Kielland
Alexandre Dumas
Alfred Gatty
Alfred Ollivant
Alice Duer Miller
Alice Turner Curtis
Alice Dunbar
Allen Chapman
Alleyne Ireland
Ambrose Bierce
Amelia E. Barr
Amory H. Bradford
Andrew Lang
Andrew McFarland Davis
Andy Adams
Angela Brazil
Anna Alice Chapin
Anna Sewell
Annie Besant
Annie Hamilton Donnell
Annie Payson Call
Annie Roe Carr
Annonaymous
Anton Chekhov
Archibald Lee Fletcher
Arnold Bennett
Arthur C. Benson
Arthur Conan Doyle
Arthur M. Winfield
Arthur Ransome
Arthur Schnitzler
Arthur Train
Atticus
B.H. Baden-Powell
B. M. Bower
B. C. Chatterjee
Baroness Emmuska Orczy
Baroness Orczy
Basil King
Bayard Taylor
Ben Macomber
Bertha Muzzy Bower
Bjornstjerne Bjornson

Booth Tarkington
Boyd Cable
Bram Stoker
C. Collodi
C. E. Orr
C. M. Ingleby
Carolyn Wells
Catherine Parr Traill
Charles A. Eastman
Charles Amory Beach
Charles Dickens
Charles Dudley Warner
Charles Farrar Browne
Charles Ives
Charles Kingsley
Charles Klein
Charles Hanson Towne
Charles Lathrop Pack
Charles Romyn Dake
Charles Whibley
Charles Willing Beale
Charlotte M. Braeme
Charlotte M. Yonge
Charlotte Perkins Stetson
Clair W. Hayes
Clarence Day Jr.
Clarence E. Mulford
Clemence Housman
Confucius
Coningsby Dawson
Cornelis DeWitt Wilcox
Cyril Burleigh
D. H. Lawrence
Daniel Defoe
David Garnett
Dinah Craik
Don Carlos Janes
Donald Keyhoe
Dorothy Kilner
Dougan Clark
Douglas Fairbanks
E. Nesbit
E. P. Roe
E. Phillips Oppenheim
E. S. Brooks
Earl Barnes
Edgar Rice Burroughs
Edith Van Dyne
Edith Wharton

Edward Everett Hale
Edward J. O'Biren
Edward S. Ellis
Edwin L. Arnold
Eleanor Atkins
Eleanor Hallowell Abbott
Eliot Gregory
Elizabeth Gaskell
Elizabeth McCracken
Elizabeth Von Arnim
Ellem Key
Emerson Hough
Emilie F. Carlen
Emily Bronte
Emily Dickinson
Enid Bagnold
Enilor Macartney Lane
Erasmus W. Jones
Ernie Howard Pie
Ethel May Dell
Ethel Turner
Ethel Watts Mumford
Eugene Sue
Eugenie Foa
Eugene Wood
Eustace Hale Ball
Evelyn Everett-green
Everard Cotes
F. H. Cheley
F. J. Cross
F. Marion Crawford
Fannie E. Newberry
Federick Austin Ogg
Ferdinand Ossendowski
Fergus Hume
Florence A. Kilpatrick
Fremont B. Deering
Francis Bacon
Francis Darwin
Frances Hodgson Burnett
Frances Parkinson Keyes
Frank Gee Patchin
Frank Harris
Frank Jewett Mather
Frank L. Packard
Frank V. Webster
Frederic Stewart Isham
Frederick Trevor Hill
Frederick Winslow Taylor

Friedrich Kerst
Friedrich Nietzsche
Fyodor Dostoyevsky
G.A. Henty
G.K. Chesterton
Gabrielle E. Jackson
Garrett P. Serviss
Gaston Leroux
George A. Warren
George Ade
Geroge Bernard Shaw
George Cary Eggleston
George Durston
George Ebers
George Eliot
George Gissing
George MacDonald
George Meredith
George Orwell
George Sylvester Viereck
George Tucker
George W. Cable
George Wharton James
Gertrude Atherton
Gordon Casserly
Grace E. King
Grace Gallatin
Grace Greenwood
Grant Allen
Guillermo A. Sherwell
Gulielma Zollinger
Gustav Flaubert
H. A. Cody
H. B. Irving
H. C. Bailey
H. G. Wells
H. H. Munro
H. Irving Hancock
H. R. Naylor
H. Rider Haggard
H. W. C. Davis
Haldeman Julius
Hall Caine
Hamilton Wright Mabie
Hans Christian Andersen
Harold Avery
Harold McGrath
Harriet Beecher Stowe
Harry Castlemon
Harry Coghill
Harry Houidini

Hayden Carruth
Helent Hunt Jackson
Helen Nicolay
Hendrik Conscience
Hendy David Thoreau
Henri Barbusse
Henrik Ibsen
Henry Adams
Henry Ford
Henry Frost
Henry James
Henry Jones Ford
Henry Seton Merriman
Henry W Longfellow
Herbert A. Giles
Herbert Carter
Herbert N. Casson
Herman Hesse
Hildegard G. Frey
Homer
Honore De Balzac
Horace B. Day
Horace Walpole
Horatio Alger Jr.
Howard Pyle
Howard R. Garis
Hugh Lofting
Hugh Walpole
Humphry Ward
Ian Maclaren
Inez Haynes Gillmore
Irving Bacheller
Isabel Cecilia Williams
Isabel Hornibrook
Israel Abrahams
Ivan Turgenev
J. G.Austin
J. Henri Fabre
J. M. Barrie
J. M. Walsh
J. Macdonald Oxley
J. R. Miller
J. S. Fletcher
J. S. Knowles
J. Storer Clouston
J. W. Duffield
Jack London
Jacob Abbott
James Allen
James Andrews
James Baldwin

James Branch Cabell
James DeMille
James Joyce
James Lane Allen
James Lane Allen
James Oliver Curwood
James Oppenheim
James Otis
James R. Driscoll
Jane Abbott
Jane Austen
Jane L. Stewart
Janet Aldridge
Jens Peter Jacobsen
Jerome K. Jerome
Jessie Graham Flower
John Buchan
John Burroughs
John Cournos
John F. Kennedy
John Gay
John Glasworthy
John Habberton
John Joy Bell
John Kendrick Bangs
John Milton
John Philip Sousa
John Taintor Foote
Jonas Lauritz Idemil Lie
Jonathan Swift
Joseph A. Altsheler
Joseph Carey
Joseph Conrad
Joseph E. Badger Jr
Joseph Hergesheimer
Joseph Jacobs
Jules Vernes
Julian Hawthrone
Julie A Lippmann
Justin Huntly McCarthy
Kakuzo Okakura
Karle Wilson Baker
Kate Chopin
Kenneth Grahame
Kenneth McGaffey
Kate Langley Bosher
Kate Langley Bosher
Katherine Cecil Thurston
Katherine Stokes
L. A. Abbot
L. T. Meade

L. Frank Baum
Latta Griswold
Laura Dent Crane
Laura Lee Hope
Laurence Housman
Lawrence Beasley
Leo Tolstoy
Leonid Andreyev
Lewis Carroll
Lewis Sperry Chafer
Lilian Bell
Lloyd Osbourne
Louis Hughes
Louis Joseph Vance
Louis Tracy
Louisa May Alcott
Lucy Fitch Perkins
Lucy Maud Montgomery
Luther Benson
Lydia Miller Middleton
Lyndon Orr
M. Corvus
M. H. Adams
Margaret E. Sangster
Margret Howth
Margaret Vandercook
Margaret W. Hungerford
Margret Penrose
Maria Edgeworth
Maria Thompson Daviess
Mariano Azuela
Marion Polk Angellotti
Mark Overton
Mark Twain
Mary Austin
Mary Catherine Crowley
Mary Cole
Mary Hastings Bradley
Mary Roberts Rinehart
Mary Rowlandson
M. Wollstonecraft Shelley
Maud Lindsay
Max Beerbohm
Myra Kelly
Nathaniel Hawthrone
Nicolo Machiavelli
O. F. Walton
Oscar Wilde

Owen Johnson
P.G. Wodehouse
Paul and Mabel Thorne
Paul G. Tomlinson
Paul Severing
Percy Brebner
Percy Keese Fitzhugh
Peter B. Kyne
Plato
Quincy Allen
R. Derby Holmes
R. L. Stevenson
R. S. Ball
Rabindranath Tagore
Rahul Alvares
Ralph Bonehill
Ralph Henry Barbour
Ralph Victor
Ralph Waldo Emmerson
Rene Descartes
Ray Cummings
Rex Beach
Rex E. Beach
Richard Harding Davis
Richard Jefferies
Richard Le Gallienne
Robert Barr
Robert Frost
Robert Gordon Anderson
Robert L. Drake
Robert Lansing
Robert Lynd
Robert Michael Ballantyne
Robert W. Chambers
Rosa Nouchette Carey
Rudyard Kipling
Saint Augustine
Samuel B. Allison
Samuel Hopkins Adams
Sarah Bernhardt
Sarah C. Hallowell
Selma Lagerlof
Sherwood Anderson
Sigmund Freud
Standish O'Grady
Stanley Weyman
Stella Benson
Stella M. Francis

Stephen Crane
Stewart Edward White
Stijn Streuvels
Swami Abhedananda
Swami Parmananda
T. S. Ackland
T. S. Arthur
The Princess Der Ling
Thomas A. Janvier
Thomas A Kempis
Thomas Anderton
Thomas Bailey Aldrich
Thomas Bulfinch
Thomas De Quincey
Thomas Dixon
Thomas H. Huxley
Thomas Hardy
Thomas More
Thornton W. Burgess
U. S. Grant
Upton Sinclair
Valentine Williams
Various Authors
Vaughan Kester
Victor Appleton
Victor G. Durham
Victoria Cross
Virginia Woolf
Wadsworth Camp
Walter Camp
Walter Scott
Washington Irving
Wilbur Lawton
Wilkie Collins
Willa Cather
Willard F. Baker
William Dean Howells
William le Queux
W. Makepeace Thackeray
William W. Walter
William Shakespeare
Winston Churchill
Yei Theodora Ozaki
Yogi Ramacharaka
Young E. Allison
Zane Grey

www.ingramcontent.com/pod-product-compliance
Lightning Source LLC
Chambersburg PA
CBHW050512260626
47157CB00004B/1290

* 9 7 8 1 4 2 1 8 9 3 0 5 1 *